A FATHER'S WRATH

Fargo fired at the same split second as the would-be assassin, and the man's face dissolved in a crimson spray. The man's death wail rose loud to the sky and he pitched to the dirt, his frame racked by violent convulsions.

"Matthew!" Porter cried out, and started toward the door.

Fargo reached Porter just as he reached the threshold. Seizing hold of the back of Porter's jacket, Fargo pushed him to one side. The clan patriarch collided with a rack of dry goods and both crashed to the floor.

A shot rang out, and lead smacked into the door a handsbreath from Fargo's head.

"Damn you!" Porter raged. "That was my second-oldest son you just killed."

Fargo yelled, "He was trying to kill me!"

Porter threw a bolt of cloth off his legs and shook a fist in seething fury. "I'll see you suffer! I'll see you on your knees beggin' for your life! You'll know the torment of the damned before I'm through!"

Trembling with rage, the old man looked dead into Fargo's eyes, rose up, and charged, his fingers hooked like claws, ready to kill. . . .

THE
TRAILSMAN
#275

OZARKS
ONSLAUGHT

by

Jon Sharpe

A SIGNET BOOK

SIGNET
Published by New American Library, a division of
Penguin Group (USA) Inc., 375 Hudson Street,
New York, New York 10014, U.S.A.
Penguin Books Ltd, 80 Strand,
London WC2R 0RL, England
Penguin Books Australia Ltd, 250 Camberwell Road,
Camberwell, Victoria 3124, Australia
Penguin Books Canada Ltd, 10 Alcorn Avenue,
Toronto, Ontario, Canada M4V 3B2
Penguin Books (NZ), cnr Airborne and Rosedale Roads,
Albany, Auckland 1310, New Zealand

Penguin Books Ltd, Registered Offices:
80 Strand, London WC2R 0RL, England

First published by Signet, an imprint of New American Library,
a division of Penguin Group (USA) Inc.

First Printing, September 2004
10 9 8 7 6 5 4 3 2 1

The first chapter of this title originally appeared in *Nebraska Nightmare,* the
two hundred seventy-fourth volume in this series.

 REGISTERED TRADEMARK—MARCA REGISTRADA

Printed in the United States of America

PUBLISHER'S NOTE
This is a work of fiction. Names, characters, places, and incidents either are the
product of the author's imagination or are used fictitiously, and any resemblance
to actual persons, living or dead, events, or locales is entirely coincidental.

The Trailsman

Beginnings . . . they bend the tree and they mark the man. Skye Fargo was born when he was eighteen. Terror was his midwife, vengeance his first cry. Killing spawned Skye Fargo, ruthless, cold-blooded murder. Out of the acrid smoke of gunpowder still hanging in the air, he rose, cried out a promise never forgotten.

The Trailsman they began to call him all across the West: searcher, scout, hunter, the man who could see where others only looked, his skills for hire but not his soul, the man who lived each day to the fullest, yet trailed each tomorrow. Skye Fargo, the Trailsman, the seeker who could take the wildness of a land and the wanting of a woman and make them his own.

The Ozark Mountains, 1861—
where blood kin took on a
whole new meaning.

1

The woman's hands were tied behind her back. Her face was streaked with grime, her clothes consisted of a threadbare shirt and britches. A pretty face, Skye Fargo thought, with bright green eyes and high cheekbones and lips like ripe cherries, all framed by lustrous hair the color of corn silk.

Her captors were cut from the same homespun cloth, two rough-hewn men with features as rugged as the Ozark Mountains through which they were making their determined way. The man in the lead had a bushy, unkempt brown beard that fell in great tangles midway to his waist. A double-barreled shotgun rested in the crook of his brawny left arm.

The man bringing up the rear was younger by half, and clean-shaven. He had a rifle trained on the woman's back and was gnawing his lower lip.

Fargo's lake-blue eyes narrowed. By rights this was none of his business. He was passing through northwest Arkansas after spending a wild week in New Orleans indulging his fondness for whiskey, women, and cards. The smart thing to do was to keep riding and not interfere. But he found himself gigging the Ovaro into the open and placing his hand on the butt of his Colt. "Howdy, gents."

The bearded man halted and started to raise the shotgun but lowered it again and said in a friendly-enough fashion, "Howdy yourself, stranger." His gaze roved from the crown of Fargo's dusty white hat to the tips of Fargo's dusty boots. "We don't often see your kind hereabouts."

"My kind?" Fargo repeated. He was studying the woman, admiring how her hair cascaded over her slender shoulders and the swell of her bosom under her shirt.

"It's plain as warts on a toad that you're not hill folk," the bearded man said. "Those buckskins. That gun belt you're wearin'. Your horse and rig. You're one of those frontiersmen, or plainsmen, as some call them. What might your name be?"

Fargo told him.

"Bramwell Jackson," the man said with more than a trace of pride. "This here is my boy, Samuel. Don't let his baby face fool you. He can drop a squirrel at two hundred yards with that rifle of his."

Wondering if that was a veiled threat, Fargo nodded at the woman. "And the lady you have trussed up?"

"Is none of your concern," Bramwell flatly declared. "So I'll thank you to rein aside so we can be on our way."

"In these parts," young Samuel Jackson threw in, "folks know better than to stick their nose where it doesn't belong."

Fargo leaned on his saddle horn. "I have the same problem with my nose that you have with your mouth. Suppose you tell me why she's tied up like that? And what you aim to do with her?"

"So much for being sociable," Bramwell said. Snapping the double-barreled shotgun to his shoulder, he thumbed back the double triggers. "You'll oblige us or make your peace with your Maker."

Fargo raised his hands, palms out. All it would take was a twitch of the hillman's finger and he would be blown clean in half. "I'm not looking for trouble, mister."

"Then make yourself scarce," Bramwell advised.

"What we're doing with this gal is no more than she has comin' to her. Off you go now, or so help me, I'll turn you into a headless horseman."

Careful not to make any sudden moves, Fargo reined the Ovaro off the trail. The trio filed past, Samuel Jackson covering him with the squirrel gun until they were swallowed by vegetation. The woman never once looked back, never once said a word.

Pushing his hat back on his head, Fargo scratched his hair in puzzlement. He didn't know what to make of it. He should do as the hillman told him and continue west to the Rockies. The woman had not asked for his help. She hadn't so much as looked at him. *So why get involved?* he asked himself.

Fargo glanced in the direction he had been going, then in the direction the Jacksons and their captive had taken. "When will I learn?" he said, and reined after them. He held the stallion to a walk; he was in no hurry to ride into the twin barrels of that shotgun. There was a common saying to the effect that buckshot meant burying, with good reason. A shotgun was the next best thing to a cannon. It could splatter a man's innards from hell to heaven and back again.

The woods were quiet but that was to be expected. Birds and small animals often fell silent when their domain was invaded by man.

The undergrowth was thick, but by rising in the stirrups Fargo could see almost fifty yards ahead, enough to be forewarned of an ambush.

Evidently the hillmen were in a hurry. They quickened their pace to a brisk walk. Nor did they speak to the woman, who walked with her chin held high in silent defiance.

The terrain was typical of the Ozark Plateau, as the region was known. Steep hills, verdant valleys, and rapid streams had to be traversed. Hardwood and pine forests were the rule, broken by fertile lowlands layered with rich soil suitable for farming.

Fargo came to a wooded tract of shortleaf pines. Signs of wildlife were abundant, everything from gray and red squirrels to deer. He noticed a log that had been ripped apart by a black bear in search of grubs. A little further on he spooked a rabbit, which bounded off in long, frantic leaps.

Down one hill and up another. That was how Fargo spent the next hour and a half. Then he heard a yell and the murmur of voices, and drawing rein, he slid down, shucked his Henry rifle from its saddle scabbard, and after looping the reins around a handy limb, he cat-footed through the brush until he came to the end of the trees. He thought he would find a homestead. Instead, he beheld an entire settlement.

Over a dozen ramshackle buildings lined a dirt street that ran from south to north. Plank and log buildings cobbled together by someone who'd never heard of carpentry looked fit to collapse at the next strong gust of wind. A crudely painted sign identified a general store. Another advertised THE JACKSONVILLE SALOON.

Other than a lone mule at a hitch rail, there were no signs of life. Fargo figured the heat of the afternoon sun had driven most of the inhabitants indoors.

The saloon door opened and out strolled Bramwell Jackson. A much older man accompanied him and produced a plug of tobacco. They each took a bite and chewed, their cheeks bulging, and talked in hushed tones.

Fargo circled to the left to come up on the saloon from behind. He intended to find out what became of the woman and why she had been bound. Passing a gap between two houses, he spotted her at the other end, on her knees in the dirt, young Sam Jackson standing guard. Sam was staring toward the saloon and kept shifting his weight from one foot to the other.

On an impulse Fargo crept toward them. He made

4

no noise but the woman looked up and saw him. She did not smile. She did not seem relieved. She did not react in any way.

"I want you to know I don't like this much," Sam Jackson said, glancing at his charge. "But since you joined the rebels, I reckon it's fittin'."

"Oh sure," the woman angrily spat. "Blame the women. Isn't that always the way?"

"Don't start with me, Clover," Sam said. "I'm only doing what I'm told." He let out a long sigh. "You'll be lucky if they let you off with a hundred lashes with a bullwhip."

Clover shifted and glared. "Why don't the elders just up and hang me? They'll have one less worry."

Sam snorted. "You're peculiar, even for a female. Count your blessin's you're still breathin'."

By then Fargo was close enough to touch the Henry's muzzle to the back of Sam Jackson's neck. "Not a peep," he whispered. "Not so much as a twitch." Fargo half expected the young man to shout a warning to Bramwell but Sam stood stock-still, his mouth clamped shut. Reaching around, Fargo relieved him of the rifle. "Back up. Nice and slow."

Once Sam was out of sight of the saloon, Fargo made him lie facedown on the ground with his hands behind his back. He removed the younger man's belt and used it to bind Sam's wrists. The belt was old and cracked and wouldn't hold him for long but Fargo needed only enough time to reach the Ovaro.

"You shouldn't be doing this, mister," Sam broke his silence. "You have no idea what you're mixin' into."

"I couldn't just ride off," Fargo said.

"My pa will be furious. So will grandpa. They'll come after you, mister. Mark my words."

"Let them." Removing his bandanna, Fargo paused. There was something he had to know. "What did this woman do? Is she wanted by the law?"

5

"No, nothin' like that," Sam said. "She made the mistake of gettin' the leader of our clan good and mad."

"That's all? Open wide," Fargo said, and when the young man obeyed, he stuffed the bandanna into his mouth. "In case you get any ideas about yelling for help."

Sam coughed a few times, then breathed noisily through his nose.

Turning to Clover, Fargo was surprised to find her still on the ground. "I can get you out of here."

"Why should I go with someone I don't know? Someone I never set eyes on until today?"

Her answer was another surprise. "It's either that or the bullwhip," Fargo said, which goaded her into rising and coming over. Bending, he drew his Arkansas Toothpick from its ankle sheath inside his right boot and set to work on the rope around her wrists. "What exactly did you do?"

Clover stared at Sam Jackson and did not answer.

"Suit yourself." Fargo wrapped a long piece of rope around Sam's ankles and knotted it. "There. That should buy us the time we need." Taking hold of Clover's warm hand, he hurried into the trees. "Anyplace I can take you?"

"No."

Fargo was growing annoyed with her attitude. "You might at least thank me."

"For what? Being an idiot?"

Fargo stopped and looked at her but before he could ask her to explain herself, there was a shout from the settlement. Bramwell had found his son and was bellowing for others to come on the run.

"Let's light a shuck." Fargo ran the rest of the way. Vaulting into the saddle, he lowered his arm. "Up you go."

Clover hesitated. "I don't see why you're going to

6

all this bother." But she permitted him to swing her up behind him.

"Hold on," Fargo cautioned, and applied his spurs. They broke from the underbrush and he brought the Ovaro to a gallop. Her arms slid around his waist and clamped tight, her cheek rested on his shoulder blade.

"There they go!" someone hollered.

A shot shattered the tranquil woodland and lead smacked into a tree trunk. Looking back, Fargo glimpsed riders already giving chase. He reined left, threading through the boles with a skill born of long experience. No more shots rang out, and after a while the dull thud of hooves faded. Soon he felt safe in slowing so to not unduly exhaust the stallion. He glanced at Clover, who had her eyes shut and was scowling. "Are you all right?"

"Never better." Her sarcasm was thick enough to cut with a blunt table knife. "Stop and put me down. I can find my own way from here."

"Not until you tell me what that was all about," Fargo said. A reasonable request, in his estimation, after his efforts on her behalf.

"When goats sing." Clover opened her eyes and straightened. "Fargo, is it? I suppose I should be grateful, but all you've done is brought more grief down on my head. The elders will be madder than ever."

"The who?"

"The elders. They run things. Run Jacksonville. The rest of us must abide by their decisions or else." Clover paused. "Usually."

Although Arkansas was a full-fledged state, parts of it were as wild and wooly as the untamed territories west of the Mississippi River. Federal marshals were too few and too scattered to be counted on, and many counties had yet to appoint sheriffs. Settlements like Jacksonville had to deal with lawbreakers as best they were able. "Why are they out to punish you?" Fargo asked.

"I spoke my mind," Clover said. "Happy now?"

"Since when is that a crime?" Fargo was listening for sounds of pursuit but so far he had not heard any.

"Since Porter Jackson took it into his head that he's the Almighty," Clover said bitterly. "He founded Jacksonville nigh on twenty years ago, and he lords it over everyone as if it were his God-given right."

Several questions occurred to Fargo but just then hoofbeats drummed in the distance. Once more he brought the Ovaro to a gallop, once more Clover had to cling tight. She clung so hard, in fact, that he could feel the enticing swell of her breasts against his back.

"You'll never outrun them," Clover said in his ear. "They know this country a heap better than you."

"Maybe so," Fargo acknowledged, "but I won't make it easy for them." So saying, he plunged down one slope and up another, skirting thickets by a hairsbreadth, avoiding boulders by a whisker. At the top of the next hill he drew rein and scanned the countryside to their rear.

"Look there!" Clover exclaimed, pointing.

Fargo had already seen them. Six riders, coming hell-bent for leather. In the lead was a burly slab of muscle with a big brown beard.

"Bramwell will never forgive you for shamin' his son like that," Clover said. "He's right proud of his pups, Sam most of all."

Wheeling the Ovaro, Fargo descended the hill and traveled half a mile to a wooded rise dotted with deadfall. A game trail offered a way to the top and he took it, expecting another slope on the far side. Instead, he came to a stop at the edge of a bluff over a hundred feet high. Below were jagged rocks and the bleached skeleton of a buck, stubs of its antlers still attached to the skull.

"Is there a way down?" Clover asked.

Fargo leaned as far out as he dared, clinging to the saddle horn with one hand, his right boot nearly out of the stirrup. "Not that I can see."

"That's too bad."

"Don't worry," Fargo assured her. "I'll turn around and we'll be long gone before Bramwell gets here."

Clover put her hands on his shoulders. "No. I meant it's too bad for you. You deserve better after being so nice and all."

"I don't understand," Fargo said. The next moment he did; she shoved him with all her might while simultaneously kicking his right leg free of the stirrup. Before he could so much as blink, he plummeted over the brink.

2

"No! I—" Clover cried out.

Fargo did not hear the rest. Flinging out his hands, he clutched at a boulder but could not quite catch hold and the next moment he was tumbling down the bluff like an uprooted tumbleweed. Jarring pain speared his left shoulder. A pang shot up his right leg. He glimpsed the lightning-charred stump of a long-dead tree, and twisting, he managed to wrap both arms around it and arrest his descent.

For a full minute Fargo hung there, his heart pounding in his chest. It had been close. Too close. If he had missed—the rest of the bluff was virtually sheer, with no handholds whatsoever—his bleached bones would lie amid the jagged boulders, keeping the buck's company.

From overhead came the clatter of hooves. Fargo whistled but the Ovaro did not hear him and the sounds faded. Marshaling his strength, he dug the toes of his right boot into a crack and began climbing. The utmost care was called for. One slip, one mistake, and down he would go.

Anger flared, growing with each thrust of his hands and feet. Clover had tried to kill him! Fargo had misjudged her, misjudged her badly, a lapse he would not commit twice. But as mad as it made him, he was even madder that she had stolen the Ovaro. West of the

Mississippi it was a hanging offense, and with good reason. A man on foot was easy prey for every savage beast or hostile war party he met.

Fargo reached up, found a pocket from which a stone had been dislodged, and wedged his fingers into it. Using his left boot to lever higher, he was about to extend his right arm and seek another purchase when the pocket of dirt broke apart under the pressure.

For harrowing seconds Fargo teetered, his entire weight on his left foot. A strong gust of wind would send him hurtling to his death. Then his frantic, questing fingers found a rocky knob the size of his fist, and after steadying himself, he climbed with renewed urgency.

At the top he hooked his elbows onto the lip to pull himself high enough to wriggle like a salamander until his knees cleared the edge and he could stand. His sigh of relief was heartfelt.

There was no sign of the Ovaro. Its tracks led into the trees. Fargo bent his steps in the same direction. Since the Henry was still in its saddle scabbard, he was left with the Colt and the Arkansas Toothpick. He wasn't entirely defenseless, which was just as well, because no sooner had he entered the woods than hooves thundered, and into view rode Bramwell Jackson and the others.

Fargo hunkered, his right hand on the Colt.

The men from Jacksonville milled their mounts about, studying the ground. Then one climbed down and crouched. He was well over six feet tall with stringy brown hair. "They stopped here a bit," he announced while reading the sign, "then went thataway." He pointed at the trees in which Fargo was concealed.

"You always were the best tracker in the family, brother Orville," said young Sam. "I bet there's none better anywhere."

Fargo knew over a dozen scouts and frontiersmen

who would put Orville to shame. Any one of them would have known at a glance that Clover had ridden off alone and he was now on foot. A second after the thought flicked across his mind, Orville bent to the ground again.

"Hold on! This is mighty strange."

"What is?" Bramwell Jackson asked.

"That stranger is on foot. Beats me why, but he's off his horse and not more than two minutes ahead of us, if that."

"Then what are you waitin' for?" Bramwell angrily gestured. "Track him down so we can see justice is done."

Fargo didn't like the sound of that. Backing into the undergrowth, he turned and ran. His spurs jangled but it couldn't be helped. He couldn't spare the time to take them off. Ducking under a low limb, he sprinted flat out for fifty yards and stopped beside a tree. Vague shapes were smack on his trail. Putting the tree between him and them, he jogged south for several minutes, then turned east. He had lost the Ovaro's tracks but he could easily pick them up again by backtracking once he shook his pursuers. *If* he shook them. They were still there, still doggedly following. "Damn," he said, and ran faster.

Fargo had to lose them, and quickly, before they caught sight of him. To that end, he stopped, sat, and hastily tugged off his boots. When he rose, he headed west, choosing the rockiest, hardest ground. In his stocking feet he left little evidence of his passing beyond a few random scuff marks.

The next time Fargo looked back the riders were no longer there. He went another quarter of a mile to be certain he had eluded them, then slipped his boots back on and made for the bluff. No matter how long it took, no matter how far he had to go, he would not rest until he recovered the Ovaro.

It was half an hour before the bluff finally hove out

of the greenery. Fargo circled to where he expected to find the pinto's tracks but none were there. Puzzled, he roved in a wide loop and discovered Clover had reined sharply west right after she rode off. She was in a hurry to get somewhere.

Fargo settled into a distance-eating dogtrot an Apache would envy. Unlike many frontiersmen, who shunned walking and running in favor of saddle leather, if he had to, he could go for hours without tiring.

Images of Clover filled his mind. Of her lovely eyes and ripe lips. Of her shapely body and the alluring contours of her long legs and thighs. Several times Fargo shook his head to dispel the tantalizing visions, but each time his thoughts returned to her more than abundant charms.

Fargo chuckled to himself. Some people had a weakness for whiskey. Some had a sweet tooth they couldn't deny. His special fondness had to do with velvet skin and heaving mounds and soft, low cries spawned in the throes of passion.

Concentrating on the tracks, Fargo wondered where Clover was heading. Home, maybe, to her parents and siblings if she had any. He hoped they wouldn't refuse to hand the Ovaro over. He had no interest in spilling blood if it could be avoided.

Presently the tracks bore to the northwest, and a hundred yards more brought Fargo to a frequently used trail marked by scores of hoof tracks and footprints. He had taken nine or ten steps when something about the footprints struck him as peculiar. He stopped and stared, trying to figure out what it was, and when it hit him, he sank onto his knee to examine them more closely. His brow knit as he traced the outline of one and then another.

As a general rule, footprints of men and women differed. Women had smaller, more slender feet, and left smaller, more slender tracks. There were exceptions, of course, but Fargo was willing to stake his reputation as one of the army's best scouts that almost all the recent footprints before him had been made by the fairer gender. Only one set of tracks belonged to a man. That was damned strange.

Another strange fact was that the majority of the tracks pointed northwest. Only half as many came the other way.

Fargo rose and resumed jogging. His left leg was a little stiff and he was caked with sweat. A bend appeared and he started around it, mopping his forehead with his sleeve. For a few seconds his eyes were not on the trail. Lowering his arm, he instantly froze. Those seconds had proven costly.

"Sister Clover was right," said a buxom beauty with a cold face who had just stepped from the undergrowth with a leveled rifle in her hands. "She said a handsome hombre would show up, and here he is." Her thumb moved and there was a *click*. "Pretend you're a tree if you know what's good for you, stranger."

"Cover him, Sister Prudence." A brunette had emerged from the vegetation on the other side of the trail. Holding a cocked Remington revolver, she sidled warily around to relieve him of his Colt.

"He looks like he's well-trained, Sister Evangeline," said the other, her mouth upturned in a smirk. But there was nothing playful about the cold glint in her hazel eyes, or how her finger was curled around the rifle's trigger.

Fargo made no sudden moves. "All I want is my horse," he told them.

Past them the trail turned again. They had picked the perfect spot to waylay anyone coming along. "Clover stole him."

"*Borrowed* is more like it," Prudence said.

"Horses are scarce in this neck of the woods," Evangeline added. "Especially for those of the female persuasion."

"How's that again?" Fargo asked, but instead of receiving an answer, Evangeline prodded him with her revolver. "Start walkin', outsider. And don't think I won't put a hole in you if you act up."

Their clothes, Fargo noticed, were shabby homespun, the same as Clover's. And like her, they wore shirts and pants instead of dresses. "Would either of you like to tell me what this is all about?"

"No," Evangeline said, and prodded him harder.

Containing his annoyance, Fargo continued along the trail. Part of him was galled by their treatment but he was also plenty curious. "Have I stumbled on a feud?" he fished for information. "Your family against the Jacksons?"

"Oh, there's a feud, all right," Evangeline said, "but not the kind you think. This one has been brewin' since the Garden of Eden."

Fargo had no idea what to make of that comment. He tried again. "Why did Clover turn on me when I was only trying to help her?"

"You'll have to ask her," Evangeline said. "Now quit flappin' your gums. We never know when one of them might pop out at us and I don't have a hankerin' to spend a month or more in the pit."

"The pit?" Fargo quizzed her, and received a rap on the back of his head that nearly knocked his hat off.

"Hush up, dang you. You're worse than my grandma. She can gab your head off without takin' a breath."

Beyond the next bend the trail angled down a grassy slope into a long, lush valley bisected by a meandering blue ribbon. Some forty head of cattle grazed contentedly. Midway across a cluster of buildings had sprouted.

Over a dozen children were playing amid a stand

of trees. All girls, Fargo noticed. Near a corral flanking a barn were several adults. In front of the barn, and over by the house, were more women. Forgetting himself he asked, "Aren't there any men here?"

"Not if they want to go on breathing," was Evangeline's enigmatic reply.

"Us Amazons don't take kindly to your kind."

"Amazons?"

"There you go again, leaky mouth. I swear, if I had a needle and thread, I'd sew your lips shut." Evangeline jabbed him between the shoulder blades.

Fargo resigned himself to waiting for the answers he needed. He grinned when he beheld the Ovaro tied to a hitch rail. The pinto pricked its ears and stamped the ground.

"Looks like your critter is right pleased to see you," Evangeline commented. "If it only knew."

The women by the corral and the barn were coming over. More were filing from the house. Among them was Clover, her features downcast. But it was the woman in the lead who piqued Fargo's interest the most. She was a walking wall, barely five feet tall and almost as wide, with arms and legs as stout as logs and a face that would scare a grizzly. She, too, wore a shirt and pants, but hers were store-bought. So was the broad leather belt she wore. From it hung a Smith and Wesson.

"So this is the buckskin Lothario?" Her voice reminded Fargo of the bellow of a moose. She had small, piggish eyes, and more hair on her upper lip than most women were comfortable with. "Aren't you glad you didn't kill him, Sister Clover?" She asked with barely concealed contempt.

"Yes, Sister Argent," Clover answered, her gaze fixed on the ground and not on Fargo.

"You shouldn't be," Argent said. "He's one of *them,* isn't he? One of our mortal enemies?"

Fargo cleared his throat. "Lady, I've never set eyes on you before. I'm not your enemy unless you want me to be." He smiled to show his friendly intentions and was completely unprepared for the powerful backhand Argent delivered. She slapped him so hard it rocked him on his heels. Momentarily riveted in surprise, he balled his fists but froze when rifles and revolvers were brandished by nearly every woman present.

Argent grinned in sadistic delight. "Oh, look, sisters! We have a he-bear on our hands! A man with grit!"

"You had no cause to do that," Fargo said between clenched teeth.

"You're male," Argent responded. "That's all the excuse any of us need." Laughing, she drew the Smith and Wesson and pointed it at his face. "Maybe you would like to take a swing at me?"

Clover placed her slim hand on the heavier woman's thick wrist. "He's not from around here. We shouldn't involve him. Please."

Fargo was at a loss. First the blonde tried to kill him, now she was pleading for his life. He didn't know what to make of her.

"Where he's from has no bearing," Argent said testily. "It's what he *is* that counts. And it's *Sister* Argent, if you don't mind."

Realizing he would get nowhere with her, Fargo looked at Clover. "You owe me. The least you can do is explain what this is all about."

Argent raised her hand as if to strike him again. "She doesn't owe you a damn thing, mister. Count your blessings you're still alive. Because you might not be for long, not if your trial ends as I expect."

"Trial?" Fargo was making a habit of repeating what they said. "I haven't broken any laws." He had an urge to break through them to the Ovaro, yank the Henry from the saddle scabbard, and teach them a thing or three. But the conviction he would be riddled before he got off a shot dissuaded him.

"That's where you're wrong, stranger," Argent was saying. "You *have* done something wrong. You were born."

"You're making no damn sense at all," Fargo muttered. He would dearly love to wipe the sneer off her face but he deemed it best to play along until a chance to escape arose.

"Do you hear him, sisters?" Argent asked her companions. "Typical male arrogance. How about if we teach him some humility? How about if we put him on trial, and afterward we can hang him from the old oak out back of the barn?"

Many of the women laughed and nodded.

The world had gone stark loco, Fargo reflected, and he was caught up in the madness.

3

A sparkling shaft of sunlight pierced a gap between two warped boards and fell across Fargo's face. The sun was setting. In another hour darkness would descend, and he couldn't wait.

Scowling, Fargo sourly regarded his surroundings. The reek was terrible. The women had stuck him in a chicken coop, of all things, and left him under guard while the rest went to debate his fate. Their voices drifted from an open window in the farmhouse. From the sound of things, Argent and Clover were arguing heatedly over whether or not he should be set free. Well, he had a say in that, and just as soon as the sun went down, he was getting the hell out of there.

A nervous *cluck-cluck-cluck* from across the coop reminded Fargo of the seven roosting hens. They weren't any happier than he was about him being there, and kept turning their heads and eyeing him as if he were a fox about to pounce. Their constant clucking was grating on his nerves. He looked down at the floor for something to throw but it was covered with straw and droppings. "You're lucky I don't pluck one of you and eat you raw," he growled, and one of the hens squawked.

Fargo was in a foul mood. He had put up with all the stupidity he could abide. Women or no, they had no right to hold him like this. Argent's repeated threats to hang him had only fueled his resentment.

Outside, the woman standing guard leaned against the door and yawned. Fargo still had no idea why they were holding him and he didn't much care. But since he had nothing better to do, he moved closer and asked, "What's your name?"

The young woman stiffened and sprang back as if he had poked her with his knife. "I'm not supposed to talk to you, mister." She wasn't much over twenty, with long black hair and high cheekbones.

"What can it hurt?" Fargo asked, keeping his voice low so no one in the house would hear.

"Argent wouldn't like it."

"And you always do what she tells you, is that how it goes? She bosses the rest of you around as she sees fit?"

"No one bosses me," the woman declared, then cast an anxious look at the farmhouse and whispered, "My name is Lavina."

"Mind telling me what this is all about?" Fargo coaxed. "A condemned man has the right to know why he's been condemned."

"If I do, Argent is liable to be upset with me."

"There you go again," Fargo said, and smiled when she glanced at the gap through which he was talking. She had eyes almost as blue as his, and her shirt and pants clung to her like sculpted wax.

"You don't understand. None of us really want to hurt you. Well, except for Sister Argent. But she hates men on general principle. If it were up to her, there wouldn't be any."

"A world of women," Fargo said, and winked at her through the crack. "I wouldn't mind being the last man left alive. But not the first to go."

"Oh, you're not the first—" Lavina said, and caught herself.

"You've killed others?" Fargo had regarded the whole affair as little more than misguided silliness, but now it acquired a new, decidedly darker dimension.

Lavina said hastily, "Not me personally, no, but—" Again she stopped. Again she glanced at the farmhouse. "I can't. I'm truly sorry but I just can't."

"Put yourself in my boots. You know I'm not from around here. Is it too much to ask that someone tell me what in hell is going on?"

"I don't blame you for being angry. I would be too." Lavina gnawed on her lower lip, then stepped close to the crack. "All right. You deserve that much. You made the mistake of being in the wrong place at the wrong time."

"It was wrong of me to help Clover?"

"No, not at all. That was awful decent. I only meant that you've blundered smack into the middle of a war that's been wagin' for months now, with no sign of it endin' any time soon." Lavina did not sound happy about it.

"Strange I haven't seen army troops anywhere," Fargo dryly commented.

"It's not that kind of war," Lavina clarified. "This one is different." She paused. "This is a war between women and men."

Fargo simply stared. It never failed, he thought. Just when he figured he had heard every preposterous notion there was, along came someone with something so idiotic, it defied belief. "You're serious?"

"Never more so. Four women have been murdered and more of our blood will be spilled before it ends. Mark my words."

"How did it start?"

Before Lavina could answer, the back door to the house opened and out strode Argent, others in her wake. Lavina promptly turned and leaned on her rifle and pretended to be interested in the sunset.

"Did my eyes deceive me? Were you just talking to him?" Argent demanded. "After I expressly forbid it?"

Lavina shook her head. "I would never go against

your wishes, you know that, Sister Argent. He wanted food and water, is all."

Argent placed her big hands on her broad hips and bobbed her double chin at the chicken coop. "Open the door."

The other women spread out. Clover was with them, armed with a rifle like the rest. But she was the only one who didn't wedge it to her shoulder when Fargo emerged and brushed pieces of straw from his shirt.

"What now, ladies? Do you still plan to make me do a strangulation jig?" Fargo would go down fighting before he would let them place a rope around his neck.

"As much as I would like to," Argent said, "I've been persuaded to be lenient. You get to ride out so long as you agree to our conditions."

Fargo glanced at Clover but she wouldn't meet his gaze. "What might they be?" He considered wresting a rifle from the nearest woman, but now that they were letting him go, there was no need.

"You're to leave and never come back. If we ever spot you in our neck of the woods again, we'll shoot you on sight. You can take your horse but your rifle and pistol stay with us," Argent recited.

"I'm not going anywhere without my guns." It wasn't that Fargo couldn't buy others. It was the principle of the thing.

"In case you haven't noticed," Argent said, "you don't have a say. We hold all the high cards. You'll do as we tell you or learn to breathe dirt."

Clover broke in with, "Please, mister, do as she wants. You're gettin' off easy. If you were a Jackson you would be buzzard bait by now."

Outnumbered and surrounded, Fargo had no choice but to let them usher him around the house to the hitch rail. More women and a number of small girls watched from the front porch. Unwrapping the reins, he placed a boot in the appropriate stirrup and swung up, the saddle creaking as he straightened.

"Remember," Argent warned, "don't let us catch you anywhere in these mountains or you'll regret it." She gripped the bridle. "Were it up to me, we would keep your horse, too. But the others are feeling generous after what you did for Sister Clover." Pointing toward the trail out of the valley, she said, "Fan the breeze. And remember. We'll have you covered the whole time."

Fargo wheeled the Ovaro and jabbed his spurs. He was boiling inside. They were running him off like a whipped cur with its tail between its legs. No one had ever done that to him before and he did not like it one little bit.

It wasn't that they were women. Fargo had never been one to think of females as inferior, as a lot of men were prone to do. It was being *run off* that grated. He had never backed down from anyone or anything in his life, and he would be damned if he would start now.

He shifted in the saddle. They were staring after him, many with their rifles aimed at his back. Movement in some maples he was passing alerted him to a lookout he had not noticed on the way in, a sandy-haired girl with a squirrel gun. She grinned at him, the squirrel gun fixed on his torso.

Grazing cattle moved out of his way. A calf frolicked close to the Ovaro but pranced off again. Soon Fargo came to the trail head. He wasn't at all surprised when he rode around the bend and there were Prudence and Evangeline, waiting. "Ladies," he said, touching his hat brim. "I can't say it's been fun."

Prudence motioned with her rifle. "Just keep ridin', outsider," she gruffly commanded.

"We're just following orders," Evangeline said. "I'm sorry we had to treat you as we have."

"Quit grovelin'," Prudence snapped. "We don't owe him an apology. He's male, ain't he? That's reason enough."

Fargo rode on around the next bend. Breaking the stallion into a trot, he traveled for a quarter of a mile, then veered into the underbrush. He had gone far enough; he was out of sight and out of earshot.

The sun had relinquished its fiery reign to the cool of night and a myriad of stars sprinkled the firmament when Fargo climbed down and tied the reins to a sapling. Bending, he removed his spurs and placed them in his saddlebags. Then he turned and cat-footed back the way he came. A sliver of moon rose to the east, providing enough light for him to go faster.

He heard the two women before he spotted them, seated cross-legged under a tree. They thought him long gone and were at ease, their rifles across their legs. Crouching, he crept through the undergrowth until he was close enough to overhear.

"—handsome devil, I'll grant you that," Prudence was saying. "But we couldn't let his looks sway us."

"A girl could lose herself in those eyes of his," Evangeline breathed. "And those shoulders! I'll see him in my dreams from now on."

"Hussy," Prudence said, but she was grinning. "Don't let Sister Argent catch you talkin' like that or she'll have you on kitchen duty for a month."

Evangeline shrugged. "Let her. I'm tired of spendin' hours every day out here waitin' for an attack that never comes."

"It will," Prudence said. "Bramwell and his father won't take this lyin' down. Their authority has been challenged. They'll by God crush us or die tryin'."

"So Sister Argent keeps sayin'," Evangeline commented. "But between you and me, she's so smitten with herself, she wouldn't know the truth if it jumped up and bit her on her big ass."

Prudence glanced toward the valley and put a finger

to her friend's lips. "Hush, consarn it. Our relief will be here any minute, and if they were to hear you and report back to her, she might banish you."

"I don't care if she does," Evangeline said. "I refuse to be scared of her, like some are. She's a woman, same as us."

"But one who can lift you over her head and snap your spine across her knee without half tryin','' Prudence said. "She's stronger than most men I know."

Fargo wanted to hear more but just then footsteps pattered lightly in the gloom and around the bend came two women, rifles cradled in their arms. The dark hid their faces so he did not recognize Clover until she spoke.

"Sorry we're late. Argent was rakin' me over hot coals." Clover leaned her rifle against the tree. Burnished metal gleamed in the starlight, and Fargo gave a start. It was his Henry. "You would think I let myself be taken on purpose, the way she carries on."

"She hates it when things don't go how she'd like them to go," Evangeline said. "Which is why we'll be stuck in this valley until hell freezes over."

Prudence stood. "Quit talkin' like that. You know how much I miss my husband. I'd as soon this whole mess was over and done with so things can go back to how they were. The sooner, the better."

"Maybe things will never be the same," Evangeline said forlornly. "Maybe we've gone too far, what with the killin's and all."

"Are you comin' with me?" Prudence had started up the trail. "Or are you content to sit out here all night feelin' sorry for yourself?" The inky veil swallowed her and she was gone.

"Wait for me!" Evangeline yelped, shooting to her feet. "You know I don't like walkin' in the dark alone." She bounded off, saying over her shoulder, "You girls keep your eyes skinned. We don't want your throats slit like the others."

25

Fargo was in motion the moment the brunette disappeared. As silently as a wraith, he stalked toward the tree, toward the Henry. It was a stroke of luck, Clover bringing it, and he would make the most of fate's whim.

The woman who had accompanied Clover sat in the same spot Prudence had, and leisurely stretched. "What do you say we take turns? Wake me in four hours and I'll spell you."

"We're not supposed to sleep when we're standin' watch," Clover said.

"Since when did you become a stickler for followin' Sister Argent's orders? Sneakin' off on your own like that was far worse than catchin' forty winks."

"I had to try to mend fences, Harriet. This war has gone on long enough. I thought Bramwell would listen to reason but he has hardened his heart against us. He took me straight to his pa to be judged."

Invisible in the shadows, Fargo was only fifteen feet from the tree. He slowed, placing each boot with deliberate care. Once he got his hands on the Henry, there would be an accounting.

Harriet placed her rifle beside her legs and laced her fingers behind her head. "You were graspin' at straws. The men don't want peace restored. They want to lord it over us like always." She yawned and her chin dipped to her chest. "Now be a dear and be quiet so I can get some sleep."

Fargo abruptly halted and hunkered. Movement had registered off in the woods. Something, or someone, was out there. Grass rustled, and a twig snapped.

Clover was instantly alert. "Did you hear that?"

"Will you relax?" Harriet rejoined. "I didn't hear a thing. It's your nerves playin' tricks on you."

She could not have been more wrong. Out of the dark rushed four stealthy shapes, and before Clover or Harriet could think to cry out, they were seized and flung bodily to the ground.

4

Fargo was about to spring from concealment when a fifth and then a sixth shape materialized on the other side of the trail, their rifles glinting in the moonlight. He stayed where he was. So far he had gone unnoticed and he would like to keep it that way.

Harriet was resisting with the fierce frenzy of a bobcat, kicking and biting and struggling mightily. But she was no match for the two men on top of her, and her arms and legs were soon pinned.

Strangely enough, Clover did not lift a finger to defend herself. She gave up as docilely as a week-old kitten.

Both women were hauled to their feet and half dragged, half carried over to the pair by the trail.

"Cousin Clover," Bramwell Jackson said grimly. "As I told you before, there is no escape from us this side of the grave." Turning, he clamped his hand onto Harriet's chin. "And you, cousin. How will you justify your betrayal when you're taken before the judgement seat?"

"I did what I believed was right," Harriet answered.

"You turned on your own kin. Worse, you and all those other misguided females now stand accused of seven counts of foul murder."

"*Us?*" Harriet screeched. "What about the four women that you and yours have sent to their reward?"

"I have no idea what you're talkin' about," Bramwell said.

"Liar! Is there no end to your wickedness?" Harriet shook her head in disgust. "If anyone is to blame, it's your high-and-mighty father, not us."

Bramwell's hand was a blur. There was the sharp *crack* of a powerful slap, and Harriet's head snapped back. He raised his arm to strike her again but Clover intervened.

"Enough! Punish us if you think you must, but not like this. Beatin' us only proves we've been right all along."

Bramwell still might have struck Harriet again if not for young Samuel, who lowered his rifle and clutched his father's sleeve.

"Don't do it, Pa. She's right. We have no call to hurt them."

"Unhand me, son," Bramwell said sternly. "They've given us all the cause in the world. The problem is, they won't accept the consequences of their actions." He placed a hand on Sam's shoulder. "But I shouldn't be surprised you would take their side. You've always been too soft. I blame your mother. She wouldn't let me be as strict as I should have when you were a boy."

"You were plenty strict," Sam said.

"I spared the rod too many times at her insistence. Iron is forged in a furnace, not in a field of flowers." Bramwell gestured. "This isn't the time or place to talk about that right now. We have more important matters to attend to."

Fargo's Henry was still propped against the tree. So tantalizingly close, he started to slink toward it but froze again when one of the men turned and gathered up the weapons. The others bound Clover's and Harriet's arms behind their backs.

"What now?" Clover asked. "You'll never reach the farmhouse. We're not the only lookouts. Even if you did, Argent and the rest will put up a fight, and there aren't enough of you to beat them."

"I wouldn't think of tryin'," Bramwell said. "Not yet, anyhow. Rest assured that when the time comes, every last male kin you have will take part."

The hillmen led their two captives back up the trail in single file.

Unknown to them, they had company. A dozen yards into the vegetation, Fargo kept silent pace. They had left their horses a lot closer than the Ovaro, and after they mounted and rode off, with Clover and Harriet forced to ride double, Fargo raced to the Ovaro and lit out in pursuit. He had gone about a mile when he spotted them in the distance. He stayed well back so as not to give himself away, stopping often to look and listen. He assumed they would ride all night in order to reach Jacksonville by dawn but along about midnight flames leaped to life, forewarning him they had stopped and made camp.

Drawing rein, Fargo dismounted and slunk the rest of the way on foot. He covered the last fifty yards on his elbows and knees. A coffee pot had been put on to boil, and all the men save one ringed the fire. The exception was by the horses, standing guard.

The women were curled on their sides, the firelight playing over their anxious faces.

"You're takin' a risk," Clover said. "The others will come after us."

"I happen to know Argent only has four horses left," was Bramwell's calm reply. "Our raid last week was a success." His busy beard parted in a mocking grin. "At any rate, you won't be missed until daylight. We'll reach Jacksonville long before they can reach us."

"You have it all figured out," Clover bitterly remarked. "Typical. Porter and you always think you know everything."

"Oh, please," Bramwell said. "Your petty spite is uncalled for. We're not the ones who started this ruckus. We're not the ones who broke four hundred years of clan tradition."

"What holds in the Old Country doesn't hold here," Clover said. "This is the New World. New ways. It's high time you and your pa realize that."

Fargo was searching for the Henry. None of the men by the fire had it. Nor was it on the ground or propped on a saddle.

"That's not you talkin'," Bramwell said. "That's Argent Meriwether puttin' words in your mouth."

"Amen to that," echoed Orville.

"You blame her for openin' our eyes?" Clover arched her eyebrows. "For showin' us the difference between right and wrong."

"No, I blame myself for ever agreein' to your loco notion about hirin' a schoolmarm," Bramwell said. "Pa and I should have known better. But you've always had a persuasive tongue, Clover Jackson. Too damn persuasive for our own good." He suddenly turned. "Samuel, you're awful quiet tonight. Something eatin' at you, boy?"

"Nothin', Pa," Sam said with a complete lack of sincerity.

"What have I told you about lyin'?" Bramwell snapped. "Your ma and me raised you better, God rest her soul."

The hillman guarding the horses was pacing back and forth to keep awake, judging by his repeated yawns. His next step brought him near enough to the fire for Fargo to recognize the rifle he was holding: the Henry. Fargo began circling the string, glad the wind had died so the horses wouldn't catch his scent.

Sam squirmed like a worm on a hook, then reluctantly said, "I just don't like this, Pa. I don't like what's become of us. I don't like all the killin' and everyone hatin' everyone else."

"And you think I do?" Bramwell indignantly asked.

"Of course not. But the feud has gone on too long. We have to return things to how they were."

It was Clover who spoke. "Wishful thinkin', cousin. We can never go back to the old ways. Once a person has seen the light, they can't go back to livin' in darkness."

"How dare you?" Bramwell bristled. "Who is that vile creature to say she's right and our clan is wrong?" He smacked the knotty knuckles of his right fist against his calloused left palm. "She's an abomination! A deceiver! The serpent in disguise."

There was more but Fargo wasn't listening. He had eyes and ears only for the guard, whose pacing had brought him to within easy arm's reach of the under-growth. Fargo tensed to spring.

Just then the guard wheeled and marched over to the fire. "How about a cup of coffee? It should be done by now and I can't hardly stay awake."

"Sure thing, Jesse," Bramwell said, and produced a tin cup, which he filled to the brim. "You can wake me in a couple of hours to spell you."

Fargo was waiting for Jesse to finish and return but Jesse lingered, taking slow sips.

Young Sam was nursing a cup of his own, his expression troubled. "Pa, what if the elders were to sit down with Meriwether and talk things out? Isn't that better than spillin' more blood?"

Bramwell scowled. "Tell me. Where is your cousin Jeb?"

"What does that have to do with anything?"

"Just answer the question," Bramwell persisted. "Where is Jeb? The closest friend you ever had?"

"He's dead," Sam said.

"And how did he die?"

"You already know. We found him with his throat slit from ear to ear, lyin' in a pool of his own blood."

"And your cousin Franklyn? Where is he?"

"Dead."

"And your cousin Luther? And Enosh? And Malachi? And Thomas?"

"Dead, dead, dead, and dead," Samuel said. "But that doesn't mean we can't put an end to the war."

"It sure as hell does," Bramwell disagreed. "Would you have us tarnish their memory by lettin' their killer go free? I certainly hope not. I'd disown you in a heartbeat if I ever thought you would stoop so low."

Clover was struggling to sit up. "Wait a minute. Did I hear correctly? All of them are dead?"

"As if you didn't know."

"And you think the women are to blame?" Clover looked in appeal to Harriet. "Tell him this is the first we've heard of it."

Just then several of the horses raised their heads and stared intently into the forest to the north. Jesse was too engrossed in the argument to notice. Nor did any of the rest. But Fargo did. His keen ears, honed to a wolfish edge by years of living on the raw frontier, detected a fleeting rustle. A bay stomped a front leg but still the hillmen paid it no mind.

"Clover is right. We haven't lifted a finger against you," Harriet said, "but your side has killed four of us. Priscilla and Tamar were the first. Knifed in the dead of night while they stood guard."

Bramwell Jackson rose. From his barrel chest rumbled a cross between a growl and a laugh. "Are you addlepated, girl? Think what you will of us, but we never, ever kill our own."

Something, or someone, was slinking toward the clearing. Fargo could not quite make it out, but from the way it moved, the newcomer was two-legged, not four. His hand automatically dropped to his empty holster, and he mentally swore.

"You're a liar, cousin Bramwell," Harriet said.

Bramwell bent to seize her. In doing so, he inadvertently saved his life, for in the foliage across the way a rifle blasted and the slug intended for Bramwell's broad back struck Jesse squarely in the sternum. It rocked him on his boot heels and burst out his back in a spray of gore. Jesse folded at the knees, dead before he struck the ground.

For a span of heartbeats everyone was rooted in profound shock. Then Harriet screamed in blind terror, even as Bramwell and Samuel and the others dived for rifles or fumbled for revolvers.

The bushwhacker fired again and Bramwell spun half around, grunting in surprise. Sam was working the lever of his rifle but it appeared to be jammed. The bushwhacker fired a third time. Not at the men, but at Harriet, who was struggling to rise, her bound hands unable to give her the boost she needed. She was only to her knees when the slug cored her right eye with a distinct, fleshy *thwack*, bored completely through her cranium, and ruptured out the rear of her skull. Her scream strangled off into a gurgling whine that ended in a pathetic whimper.

Now all the men were firing, frantically pouring rounds into the leafy verdure, shot after shot after shot, as acrid clouds of gun smoke coalesced into an artificial fog that hid the trees.

"Stop shootin'!" Bramwell Jackson roared. He had a big hand cupped to his wound and was grimacing in pain. Of all of them, he was the only one who kept his wits about him.

In the sudden silence, the crackling of the fire seemed unnaturally loud. The men fearfully raked the forest for a target. Clover was gaping aghast at Harriet, at the blood and brains oozing from the cavity where the back of her friend's head had been.

Bramwell was listening intently. "After her!" he roared, motioning with his good arm. "She can't move fast, as dark as it is!"

"She?" Clover said in bewilderment.

"Argent Meriwether, who else?" Bramwell snarled,

and motioned more violently at his son and the others. "Didn't you hear me? *After her,* damn you! We can end it once and for all." When Sam still did not move, Bramwell grabbed him by the arm and forcefully propelled him toward the benighted trees.

Reluctantly, Sam obeyed. So, too, after a few seconds' hesitation, did the others. That left Bramwell and Clover, who was unable to tear her gaze from Harriet's remains.

Fargo slowly unfolded and crept forward. Bramwell's back was to him and no one else was anywhere near. He reached the Henry and bent to pick it up. Clover saw him, though, and a sharp gasp from her caused Bramwell to whirl. Their eyes locked, and Bramwell clumsily clawed at a pistol on his hip. Fargo was quicker. In a twinkling he had the Henry centered on the unruly beard that covered Bramwell Jackson's wide chest. "At this range I can't miss."

Bramwell turned to marble, his face flushed red with wrath. "So it was you, you murderous scum!"

"No." Fargo said, but he doubted Jackson would believe him. Stooping, he hooked his other arm around Clover's waist and pulled her to her feet.

"Harriet—" Clover bleated in a horror-struck daze.

Fargo shook her. "Snap out of it. We have to get out of here." He could hear the hillmen barreling through the underbrush like so many mad bulls.

"Think so?" Bramwell Jackson crowed, and cupping his left hand to his mouth, he bellowed, "Sam! Lester! Come quick! And come shootin'! It's him! The stranger! He's here by the fire!"

From out of the shadowed woods came an answer from young Sam, "We're on our way, Pa!"

5

Fargo glanced at the woods, and the instant he did, Bramwell Jackson streaked his left hand for the revolver on his right hip. He was not particularly fast but he had it halfway out of its holster before Fargo reached him and swung the Henry. Usually, when Fargo struck someone across the head with the hardwood stock, it brought them to their knees. Not this time. All Bramwell did was stagger and then bellow with rage and lunge.

Fargo felt fingers as thick as railroad spikes clamp around his throat, choking off his breath. He wrenched to one side but Bramwell's grip did not slacken.

"Hurry! I've got him!" Bramwell's dark eyes glittered with near-maniacal bloodlust.

Loud crashing in the undergrowth told Fargo he had mere moments before the others returned. Suddenly smashing the Henry into Bramwell's groin, Fargo succeeded in doubling him over.

Wheezing and sputtering, Jackson cried, "That won't stop me, outlander!"

"Maybe this will," Fargo said, and slammed the stock against Bramwell's bull head a second time. Incredibly, although Bramwell fell to his hands and knees, he was still conscious, and glared like a gored ox.

Whirling, Fargo grabbed Clover by the arm and sped toward the beckoning sanctuary of the night-shrouded woods. They had a few steps to go when a rifle cracked and a leaden hornet buzzed uncomfortably close. Twisting, Fargo snapped off a shot from the hip just as a hillman was taking deliberate aim. It lifted the man off his feet and sent him tumbling.

Shouts heralded the others. Fargo ran, retaining a hold on Clover. She moved woodenly, overcome by shock, slowing him down considerably. Too much, as it turned out, because they were only twenty yards from the campfire when the drum of heavy footfalls revealed three of the hillmen were hard after them.

Fargo could not hope to outrun them, not with Clover so disoriented. Coming to a thicket, he skirted it, but once on the other side, he crouched and began working his way toward the center, heedless of the tiny limbs that tore at his face and hands and clung to his buckskins. Clover balked, but only until Fargo nearly pulled her off her feet.

They had crawled a yard, no more, when footfalls fell dangerously close. Fargo let go of the Henry and covered Clover's mouth in case she cried out but all she did was tremble like a fawn being chased by a pack of wolves and lean against him as if she were on the verge of collapse.

"Where did they go?" Orville Jackson shouted.

"This way!" a man bawled, and the next moment the four men barreled off in a different direction.

Fargo pressed his lips to Clover's ear and inhaled a trace of perfume. "Get hold of yourself."

"Harriet was a dear friend," Clover mewed, tears flowing, "and now she's dead."

"Unless you want to join her, don't make a peep."

Timely advice, for an inky silhouette prowled among the trees close by. It was young Sam. He came so near to the thicket that Fargo could have poked him with the Henry. But only for a few moments.

Then Sam turned and flew toward the camp and his stricken father.

Again Fargo put his mouth to Clover's ear. "My horse isn't far. Once we reach it, we're safe. Are you up to this?"

Clover gulped and nodded.

They inched from the thicket. Fargo dallied just long enough to cut the rope from her wrists. Taking her hand, he used the cover to its best advantage. At the slightest of sounds he stopped until he was sure it wasn't one of the men.

A nicker from the Ovaro greeted them. Fargo shoved the Henry into the scabbard, mounted, and swung Clover up behind him. No shouts or shots pierced the stillness as he reined northwest.

Clover's arms were around his waist, her breasts against his back. Fargo tried not to dwell on them but they were terribly distracting. He kept imagining how exquisite they must be naked. Which led him to contemplating her other charms. Fargo almost laughed aloud. Now wasn't the right time. If he wasn't careful, one day his cravings would be the death of him.

"Who was that?" Clover unexpectedly asked.

"You saw someone?" Fargo tensed and looked around. "Where?"

"Back there. Who killed Harriet? How could anyone gun her down in cold blood? She was the sweetest soul alive, and one of my best friends."

"I was hoping you might know," Fargo said. "Bramwell seemed to think it was your other friend, Argent Meriwether."

"Argent is no friend of mine," Clover said. "The day she arrived in Jacksonville was a black day in all our lives. There has been nothing but heartache ever since."

"I gathered she's not from around here," Fargo commented. Meriwether's accent, for one thing, pegged her as an Easterner.

"She's from Philadelphia," Clover revealed. "That's where she was employed when she heard about us needin' a schoolmarm."

Fargo tried to imagine Meriwether in a dress teaching tiny tots their ABCs, and couldn't. To his way of thinking, she would make a better lumberjack. He wanted to learn more but Clover's voice betrayed her fatigue and he let her lapse into silence and rest her cheek against him.

Overhead, leafy boughs swayed to the brisk breeze. The crickets were in full chorus, a musical backdrop to the thud of the Ovaro's hooves. Fargo rode for over two hours, putting enough distance behind them to eliminate any possibility of pursuit.

The gurgle of a meandering creek drew Fargo to the north and a grassy glade aglow with pale moonlight. He helped Clover down, then stripped the saddle, saddle blanket and bridle from the Ovaro. Unrolling his bedroll, he indicated his blankets. "These are for you. I'll keep watch over there." He pointed at a maple tree bordering the glade.

Clover was hunkered on her haunches, her forearms folded across her knees. "I don't want to sleep right now."

"You should." Fargo reckoned that at first light the Jacksons would be after them. "We might have a long day ahead of us tomorrow."

"There's something I need to say," Clover said. "About the bluff. About when I pushed you." She unfolded and put her hand on his, her skin warm and soft. "I didn't mean to push so hard. All I wanted was your horse so I could get away. I wasn't tryin' to kill you." She paused. "You believe me, don't you?"

"Does it matter?" Fargo asked.

"To me it does, yes." Clover gave his hand a gentle squeeze. "I treated you poorly when all you were doing was tryin' to help. My only excuse is that if you had been through the hell I have, you would understand."

"I don't savvy any of this," Fargo admitted. "Women at war with men. Everyone up in arms." He gazed off across the mountains. "The last time I came through the Ozarks, the people were as friendly as could be."

Clover stepped onto the blanket, sank down with her legs tucked, and patted a spot beside her. "Have a seat and I'll explain."

She didn't have to ask Fargo twice. He liked how her golden hair glistened, and found himself thinking about how it would feel to run his fingers through it. "About time someone did."

"It all started when a government man came through Jacksonville last summer. He said our settlement was big enough now, we should give some thought to a school. So the elders held a meetin' and put it to a vote and it was decided to build a schoolhouse and send for a schoolmarm."

Fargo liked her voice. It was low and husky and spawned ideas that had nothing to do with reading and writing.

"The government man left an address to an agency that hires out teachers and such, so Porter Jackson wrote them. I guess they keep a list of teachers lookin' for work. But the only one who answered was Argent Meriwether." Clover stopped. "I reckon the notion of teachin' in the sticks didn't appeal to most. And it didn't help that we couldn't afford to pay all that much. We thought we were mighty lucky when Miss Meriwether accepted."

Fargo knew that schools were becoming more common. Ten years ago, most schooling was done at home. Now, nearly half of all the towns and communities east of the Mississippi boasted a one-room schoolhouse. "When did the killing start?"

"I'm gettin' to that. You see, when Miss Meriwether arrived, she wasn't much taken with our ways. Called us backward right to our faces, and went on and on about how they did things in Philadelphia."

One of those, Fargo reflected. Some people had a disturbing knack for looking down their noses at anyone and everyone who didn't measure up to their standards.

"Porter and Argent tangled right off. As head of our clan, all her complaints had to go to him, and she had a lot. She wanted the schoolhouse repainted, she demanded bigger desks. And that a special fund be set up for things the school needed, like paper and ink."

"How did Porter take it?" Fargo asked. He assumed the teacher's demands had somehow led to all the trouble.

"Well enough, all things considered. He told her we didn't have a lot of money to spare but we would help out as best we could. And we did, too. We took up a collection and raised nearly two hundred dollars."

Fargo whistled. For a backwoods collection of planks and logs like Jacksonville, that was a lot of money.

"After that things calmed down for a while. Then Porter announced that Billy Jackson was takin' a wife, and Argent about threw a fit."

"You've lost me," Fargo said.

"Billy Jackson was the youngest son of Porter's youngest sister. Billy had just turned sixteen and wanted to marry Elly Jackson, the youngest daughter of Porter's youngest brother."

Fargo thought he understood. "The school teacher was upset because Billy and Elly were cousins?"

"Well, that, and the fact Elly was only twelve. We explained to Argent that it was the custom in our clan for cousins to marry cousins. And that while Elly was spoken for, the marriage wouldn't take place until she turned fourteen. But Argent went and stood in the middle of the street and denounced Porter and the elders for being what she called dirty old men. She said cousins marryin' cousins was wrong. That it was a perversion. Her exact word."

Fargo whistled again. To an outsider like Meriwether, hill folk customs must seem backward and crass. Yet those customs had endured for hundreds if not thousands of years. The Jackson clan was only doing what they had always done.

"She threatened to go to the governor until someone pointed out we weren't breakin' any laws. Then she called on Elly's mother and the rest of the women to rise in revolt, as she called it, to put the men in their place and teach them the error of their misguided ways."

"That was when the war started," Fargo guessed.

"No. None of the women wanted anything to do with her. We all thought she was plumb crazy." Clover plucked a stem of grass and stuck it between her teeth. "My own ma married when she was fourteen. So did a lot of the others. We saw nothin' wrong with what Billy and Elly were doing. Fact is, I envied her. I mean, here I am, pushin' twenty, and I still don't have a husband. Why, I'm darned near a spinster."

Fargo looked away so she wouldn't see his grin.

"Anyway, that was where things stood until Argent had a long talk with Elly's mother, Patrice, and the next thing we knew, Patrice called the weddin' off. Porter was mad enough to kick a cat. He summoned Patrice before the elders and told her she had no right to set herself against everyone else. But Patrice refused to back down."

"I still don't see how all this led to the war."

"I'm comin' to that," Clover said. "Porter and the elders decided we needed a new schoolmarm and told Argent to pack her bags and get. I guess they figured that with her gone, things would quiet down. But then Billy's and Elly's bodies were found in the old barn out back of Elly's folk's place."

Fargo's interest perked. "Someone killed them?"

"They were stabbed to death, fifteen to twenty times each, and Porter's huntin' knife was found in the straw beside their bodies."

"Why would Porter kill them?" To Fargo it made no sense. Porter was the one who agreed they should marry if they wanted.

"I can't say for certain, but Elly was startin' to come around to her mother's way of thinkin'. She told her ma that maybe Argent was right all along and she was too young to be hitched. Argent suspects that Porter killed her out of spite, and to show the rest of us women our proper place."

"Do you think that's what happened?"

Clover sighed and bowed her head. "I don't know what I believe anymore. Porter denied he had anything to do with it and ordered Bramwell to take Miss Meriwether to Fort Smith and put her on the first stage headin' east. Argent was with Patrice and several other women when Bramwell came to fetch her. Tempers flared, and someone started shootin'." She looked at him. "That's when it went from bad to worse, and the war started."

Fargo thought he heard a faint sound off in the woods but when he glanced at the Ovaro, the stallion showed no sign it had heard anything out of the ordinary. "Go on with your account."

"There's not much left. Most of the women naturally sided with Patrice and Argent and most of the men sided with Porter and Bramwell. One thing led to another, and the women ended up out at Patrice's farm while the menfolk moved into Jacksonville. Since then there has been more killin'." Clover stopped, then mustered a smile. "I feel awful sorry for you, ridin' smack into the middle of our mess like you have.

I wouldn't blame you one bit if you ride right out again."

A soft scrape from amid the trees brought Fargo to his feet. The Ovaro had raised its head and was staring fixedly into the dark.

"Is something the matter?" Clover asked.

Her answer came not from Fargo but from the woods; a rifle blasted, spraying the glade with hot lead.

6

There was no time to think. No time to speculate on who was trying to kill them. No time for Fargo to do anything other than hurl himself at Clover and bear her to the ground. He felt a tug on his sleeve and pain in his left ankle. The firing stopped, but only, he suspected, because the killer was taking better aim or moving to a better vantage point. In any event, they couldn't just lie there. Heaving Clover to her feet, he shoved her toward the other side of the glade and shouted, "Run!"

Turning, Fargo took two long strides and dived for his saddle. A shot rang out as his hands molded to the Henry. Fargo shucked it from the scabbard and snapped it to his shoulder as another shot boomed. He realized that Clover had been the target, not him. Spotting a muzzle flash, he banged off three shots of his own. Almost instantly there came the crash of undergrowth; the killer was fleeing.

Fargo gave chase. He entered the trees and spotted a darting, weaving shape. He tried to fix a bead but he could not get a clear shot. Whoever it was, they were fleet as an antelope. Try as he might, he could not narrow the gap.

Somewhere ahead a horse whinnied, and Fargo swore. He flew through a stand of saplings and burst out the other side but he was too late. Hooves were pounding eastward. He listened until the sound faded to silence, then, furious at himself, he stalked back to the glade.

The Ovaro, thank God, had not been hit. Fargo's left boot had been creased but the bullet had not penetrated the leather. "Clover?" he yelled. "Are you all right?" There was no answer, and for a few anxious seconds he feared the worst, until the vegetation parted and she ran to him and threw her arms around his neck.

"Thank you!" she breathed in his ear. "You saved me again."

The feel of her body against his stirred Fargo down low. He inhaled the scent of her hair and her body and it took all his self-control not to run his hands over her bottom. "It's becoming a habit."

Clover drew back but did not remove her arms. "Who do you reckon it was?"

"The same one who shot your friend Harriet," Fargo said. He could kick himself for not watching their back trail more closely. Apparently the killer had followed them the entire way.

"Why come after us?" Clover wondered. "Bramwell thought it was Argent but she wouldn't shoot Harriet or try to murder me. We're on her side."

It was something to ponder, Fargo reflected. But not right now. He had to remedy his carelessness. "Grab my saddle blanket and bridle."

With his saddlebags over one shoulder and his saddle in his other hand, Fargo led her into the forest. No more camping in the open until the killer was dealt with. He also brought the Ovaro in among the trees, then took the Henry and prowled in a wide circle to ensure the killer was indeed gone.

"Anything?" Clover asked when he returned.

"It's safe for you to catch some shut-eye." Fargo

sat with his back to a bole at a point where he could keep an eye on her and the stallion and see the glade, too.

"Be serious?" Clover nervously smiled and shifted her weight from one foot to the other. "I couldn't sleep now if I wanted to."

"You should try anyway," Fargo urged. "Tomorrow I'll take you wherever you want to go."

"And then you'll leave these mountains for good, I bet," Clover said. "Not that I blame you one bit."

"I'm going after whoever took those shots at us," Fargo corrected her.

Clover's lovely eyes widened. "Why? This isn't your fight. What do you care if the rest of us drown in blood?"

"You're forgetting," Fargo said. "Whoever took those shots tried to kill *me* too, and I take a thing like that personally."

"Oh." Clover sounded disappointed. "Just so you're not stayin' on my account. I don't have a man at the moment and I'm not interested in one."

A strange comment, Fargo thought, especially as he had never let on how attractive she was. Which hinted she must feel the same way about him. He decided to test the waters. "Is that men in general or husbands in particular?"

"Oh, I like men just fine," Clover admitted. "Too much so, according to a few of the older women. But sometimes something comes over me and I can't help myself. Know what I mean?"

"Down in Texas they have a saying," Fargo related. "There are two kinds of women in this world, those who are married and those who are still alive."

Clover laughed heartily. "I wouldn't go that far. It all depends on the husband, I should imagine." She pretended to be interested in the clouds. "Have you ever had a hankerin' to settle down?"

Fargo was honest with her. "I like to roam too much to ever tie myself to one spot."

"Or to one woman." Clover caught his true meaning. She shrugged. "I figured as much. A handsome gent like you must have to beat fillies off with a stick."

"I've never turned one down."

Inexplicably, Clover curled up on her side and closed her eyes. "Well, I'd best take your advice and try to get some sleep."

Fargo smothered his disappointment. She had been through a lot that day, including witnessing the horrible death of her friend. Realistically, he couldn't expect her to have the same thing on her mind as he did. With a sigh, he leaned back and placed the Henry across his legs.

Deceptive peace pervaded the night. The stars twinkled in celestial splendor, a soft wind caressed the trees, and the air was filled with the rich, dank scent of the fertile earth. But Fargo did not let it lull him into letting down his guard. He constantly scoured the woods for movement, constantly tested the wind for sound.

The Big Dipper and other constellations gradually drifted across the firmament. Midnight came and went. Clover tossed and turned a lot. Fargo chalked her restlessness up to frayed nerves and tried not to dwell on the swell of her bosom when she lay on her back.

More time passed. A bobcat stalked silently across the glade, oblivious to their presence. Shortly thereafter, in the direction the bobcat had gone, a rabbit screeched its death throes to an uncaring world.

"Consarn it," Clover suddenly said, sitting up. "I couldn't sleep if my life depended on it."

"You've been awake this whole while?" Fargo admired the play of starlight on her golden hair.

Clover stretched, arching her back delectably. "I dozed off once or twice but only for a minute or two.

Normally I have a cup of warm milk to help me relax."

Fargo made a show of patting his pockets. "I'm fresh out of cows."

Laughing, Clover stood and began pacing. "I'm bubblin' with so much energy, I can't hardly stand it. And the thing is, I have no idea why."

"We can walk some if you'd like," Fargo proposed.

"I wouldn't want to put you to any bother," Clover said. Her tone hinted differently.

Rising, Fargo relieved a cramp in his calf by flexing his leg a few times, then moved toward the creek. She fell into step beside him, so close that every few steps their elbows brushed.

"So," Clover said.

"Something on your mind?"

"Oh, no, nothin' at all," Clover answered much too quickly. "I was just thinkin' of how nice you've been to me, even when I didn't deserve it."

"I'm always nice to beautiful women," Fargo put her to the test. "And you're more beautiful than most."

Clover stopped short, then caught up again. "You're joshin'. I bet you say that to all the gals."

"No more than five or six a month," Fargo said, and was rewarded with another laugh.

"You sure know how to perk a girl's spirits. The men hereabouts aren't nearly as clever. All they care about is huntin', fishin', and guzzlin' whiskey."

"Do you hate them as much as Argent does?"

Clover was taking long strides to match his, her hips swaying suggestively. "Goodness gracious, no. I don't hate anyone. I just want the killin' to stop and things to go back to being the way they were." She frowned. "But I honestly don't know if that's possible. Too many folks have died. Too many harsh words have been said. We can't forgive if we can't forget and none of us are liable to forget this awful nightmare for as long as we're breathin'."

Fargo did not say anything.

"Although it would sure be nice to forget for a little while," Clover said quietly. "An hour or two is all I ask. Long enough to remind me of who and what I am."

Fargo still said nothing.

"I don't suppose my babblin' makes any kind of sense. Men don't look at life the way women do. Never have, never will. They can be the most stubborn cusses at times."

"Men aren't the only ones."

Clover grinned and her fingers idly stroked the back of his hand. "Land sakes. I would be the last to say that, seein' as how I'm the most stubborn person I know. When I put my mind to something, I never rest until I get what I'm after."

They came to a low bank that overlooked the softly flowing water. Fargo decided that here was as good a place as any to find out if she shared his desire for more than talk. Without saying a word, he took a seat with his legs dangling over the bank, his boots inches above the creek.

Clover hesitated, then took the bait. Sitting beside him, she clasped her arms to her chest and commented, "It's a mite chilly. I have goose bumps all over."

"We can go back," Fargo said, hinging what he did next on her answer.

"No. That's all right. I like it here. I like talkin' to you."

"Is that all?" Fargo reached up and ran his hand across her cheek and down her neck to her shoulder. She shivered, but whether from the chill or something else, he couldn't say.

Clover locked eyes with him. "I'm not that kind of girl, I'll have you know." Fargo started to pull his hand away but she grasped it in both of hers. "I still have needs, though, like everyone else."

49

"It's up to you," Fargo said.

"Does this make it plain enough?" Clover asked, and placed his hand on her right breast.

"Plenty plain." Fargo squeezed and felt her nipple harden against his palm, jutting against the fabric like a tack.

"Mmmmmm," Clover cooed. "You're off to a fine start."

Fargo bent his face to hers and hungrily glued his mouth to her yielding lips. She tensed, as if having second thoughts, then flung her arms around him, parted her mouth wide, and entwined her tongue with his in sensual yearning. He sucked on it and she moaned deep in her throat, moaned long and loud, the meantime her fingers explored his broad shoulders and chest.

When they broke for breath, Clover was panting. "My, oh my. You sure can make a girl tingle."

"I can do more than that," Fargo stated matter-of-factly, and backed up his statement by licking and nibbling on her ears and neck while his hands roamed to his heart's content.

"It's been so long!" Clover whispered, playing with his hair. "I couldn't go without much longer."

It had been Fargo's experience that women were a lot more like men than they were willing to admit. They liked a romp in the hay just as much but seldom gave in to temptation because they were afraid of the consequences.

At the moment Clover was free to give rein to her pent-up passion, and her next act was to take his chin in her hands and lavish a hundred tiny kisses and nibbles on his face and throat.

Fargo pried at her buttons until her shirt was open. Underneath were underthings he made short shrift of. The cool air on her breasts elicited a sharp intake of breath. It turned to a groan when Fargo covered her pendulous mounds with both hands and caressed and kneaded them as if they were clay. Her skin grew hot to his touch, her nipples jutted invitingly. So much so, that Fargo lowered his mouth to her right breast and fastened his mouth on the nipple. Swirling it with his tongue, he nipped ever-so-lightly and winced when her nails dug deep into his shoulders.

"Yessssss," Clover husked. "More. I want more."

Fargo aimed to give it to her. He lathered her right breast and then her left, then licked a path from between her globes to her navel. She uttered a soft cry when he rimmed it. Her hands rose to his hair and pulled so hard, he thought she would tear it out by the roots.

Taking her in his arms, Fargo moved a few feet from the creek and gently lowered her onto a natural bed of grass. She presented a torrid temptation with her lips parted seductively and her breasts glistening like ripe melons. With a quick, practiced move he had her pants off. The rest of her garments soon followed.

Clover eagerly reached up. Now that she was naked, she wanted him naked, too. Fargo helped her, and once the deed was done, knelt between her velvet thighs and parted them wide. She gripped his rigid pole, aligned it with her wet slit, and fed him into her bit by bit.

Scarcely breathing, savoring the sensation, neither of them moved, neither of them spoke. Clover finally broke the spell by groaning and slowly grinding her hips against his. Fargo responded in kind, sliding almost out and then back in, over and over and over in rising intensity and tempo until they were thrusting against one another in unchecked abandon, her small ankles locked at the small of his muscular back, her fingernails shearing into the flesh on his shoulders and arms.

Clover crested first. Arching up on the soles of her feet, she nearly raised him off the ground. Her release triggered his. The world blurred, and Fargo heard the loudest groan yet and realized it was his. When, at length, he coasted to a stop and sagged onto his shoulder beside her, she wearily grinned and pecked him on the cheek.

"Thank you. I needed that."

"Makes two of us," Fargo said, and meant it.

7

The tracks were as plain as the new day. Fargo headed out at first light, riding double with Clover. She was in fine spirits. Resting her silken blonde hair on his broad shoulder, she idly played with his ear.

"You were wonderful last night. I hope we get to do that again before we part ways."

"I should take you back to Patrice's farm." Fargo had mentioned it several times and been ignored.

"And risk that varmint gettin' away?" Clover craned forward, her breath fanning his neck. "Besides, I like your company. And I hope the feelin' is mutual."

Fargo clucked to the stallion. Arguing would be pointless. And she did have a point; if he took her to the farm, it would be hours before he took up the killer's trail. By then the bushwhacker could be half-way to Little Rock, although Fargo doubted his quarry would skip the state.

"I'll talk with the other women when I get back," Clover was rambling on. "It's high time this nonsense ended. I've known it for weeks but I have you to thank for convincin' me to do something about it."

"Me?" Fargo said.

Clover giggled. "For all their faults, men aren't the vile devils Argent paints them as. You've reminded me that men have a few good qualities, too."

"A few, huh?"

Her soft lips brushed his ear. "There's good and bad in everyone. All Argent ever does is rant about the bad. The rest of us were so upset about Elly, we let her twist our thinkin'. We let her talk us into standin' up to the menfolk when by rights we should be workin' with them to put an end to the killin'."

"It will end sooner than you think if I find the killer," Fargo vowed. He had never been one to turn the other cheek. Whoever had tried to bushwhack him would soon learn that he preferred an eye for an eye.

Clover was a regular chatterbox. "It's awful how we can become so easily led astray. Porter and the other elders might be as hardheaded as rocks but they only ever have the clan's best interests at heart. It's hardly fair to blame them for doing things the way the clan has always done them."

The killer's tracks, Fargo saw, bore to the east. But whether to the farm or to town, it was too early to tell.

"Come to think of it, none of this would have happened if not for Argent," Clover mentioned. "She stirred everyone up with that talk of hers about doing what was decent and right. But who is she to say her ways are any better than ours?" Clover gave his waist an affectionate squeeze. "Now that I've had a chance to look at things fresh, I can see I've been as wrong as wrong can be."

"That's nice." Fargo wasn't really listening. He was speculating on who the killer might be. Clover didn't think it was Argent Meriwether because Argent wouldn't shoot another woman. But maybe Harriet's death had been an accident. Maybe the killer shot her by mistake when spraying lead at Bramwell.

Then there was the bigger question of why the killer shadowed them to the glade. Fargo had the impression the killer was after Clover, and only shot at him to get him out of the way. But why her? Why not finish off Bramwell?

"I'll call them all together and propose we send someone under a white flag to the men to ask them to sit down with us and hash it out," Clover said. "A peaceable solution is still possible."

"Only if everyone wants one," Fargo interjected, "and someone sure doesn't."

"Are you suggestin' the same coyote has been behind *all* the murders?" Clover's chin rubbed back and forth across his shoulder blade, as if she were shaking her head. "That can't be."

"Why not?"

"What could the killer hope to accomplish? Other than causin' grief?"

"Your guess is as good as mine," Fargo conceded. He needed to learn a lot more before he could form an opinion.

"I think you're barkin' up the wrong tree," Clover said. "There has to be more than one person involved."

Time would tell. Fargo was grateful when she lapsed into deep thought, freeing him to concentrate on the tracks. Soon he came to where the killer had stopped for the night. Crushed grass revealed where a blanket had been spread. At dawn the killer had been up and on the move again, continuing generally east, as before.

Soon a perplexing pattern emerged. The killer had gone up one slope and down another instead of skirting the high ridges as most riders would do. As if he or she were searching for something or someone.

Along about eleven the tracks climbed to a switchback that afforded a sweeping vista in all directions. Although Fargo scoured the terrain as intently as a hunting hawk, he saw nothing other than a few frolicking sparrows and several vultures soaring high on the air currents.

The killer had reined up at the exact same spot, then gone off to the southeast at a trot. His sudden hurry had Fargo wondering if the killer had spotted them.

Toward the bottom was a belt of pines. Fargo was halfway through when a shot cracked approximately a quarter-mile away. A rifle shot that sounded a lot like the rifle the killer used.

"Hang on!" Fargo cried, and spurred the Ovaro. In his mind's eye he saw another hapless victim lying prone in a spreading pool of blood. A second shot lent fuel to his worry, and by the time he reached flat ground, the stallion was at full gallop.

Clover's cheek was tight against his back, her arms banded around his waist. When a low limb abruptly appeared, he shouted, "Duck!" They passed under it with inches to spare.

A man on horseback appeared. Fargo had only a brief glimpse and then the man was gone. But it was enough to send him flying toward the oak tree the man had been next to. Bending, he yanked the Henry out and levered a round into the chamber.

Beyond the oak was a clearing. Slowing to try and spot the killer, Fargo was taken aback when three men sprang out of nowhere. One grabbed the pinto's bridle. His right leg was seized. Then his left. Instinctively, he aimed the Henry, or tried to, because in the blink of an eye he had been unhorsed and was flat on his back with the breath knocked out of him.

Fargo sought to rise but a rifle barrel was shoved in his face even as he was relieved of the Henry. He glanced up into the spite-filled features of Bramwell Jackson. Jackson's right shoulder had been crudely bandaged. Samuel Jackson had hold of the Ovaro's bridle while another man was pulling a furious Clover from her perch.

"Let go of me, damn you!"

"Watch your mouth, woman," Orville hissed, "or so help me, I'll slap some decency into you."

Bramwell poked Fargo in the cheek. "Ask and ye shall receive. There I was, prayin' we would meet again, and you come ridin' right up as pretty as you please." He hefted the Henry. "What was that shootin' about? Were you after a deer or a rabbit? The shots led us right to you."

"That wasn't me." With startling clarity, Fargo divined who had: the killer. Whoever it was had known they were in pursuit and had spent all morning searching for Bramwell's party. That explained the killer's fondness for high lines. The shots were to lure him toward Bramwell and Bramwell toward him. It was clever, damned clever, and Fargo had fallen for it like a rank tenderfoot.

"Yes, sir," Bramwell crowed. "You blundered smack into our hands. By sunset we'll be in Jacksonville, and tomorrow you'll stand trial unless my pa decides to hang you right off."

"I wasn't part of the ambush last night," Fargo said.

"Sure you weren't," Bramwell said, and laughed. "You just happened to show up at the same time and just happened to whisk Clover away. And I was born yesterday." He nodded at the others. "Tie him."

Fargo balked at having his hands bound but with two rifles gouging his sides, what choice did he have? He was thrown, belly down, over the Ovaro, and a lead rope was looped around the stallion's neck. Sam held the other end. Behind them, another hillman led mounts bearing the blanket-shrouded bodies of Harriet and Jesse.

Clover had to ride double with Bramwell. She protested until she was red in the face but it did no good. She hit them and kicked them and called them names that turned their cheeks red, but they tied her hands and swung her up, then tied her ankles as well, linked one to the other by a piece of rope they slid under Bramwell's mount.

They had been under way for an hour when Fargo noticed young Sam repeatedly glance at him. "What?" he asked, after about the sixth or seventh time.

"Oh, I was just wonderin' how you'll look when the noose tightens around your neck," Sam said. "I hear some men turn purple and their tongues hang out."

Fargo had seen more than a few hangings. He would rather be burnt alive.

"My pa has it all figured out. Why you helped Clover escape in town. Why you helped her escape last night."

When the stripling didn't go on, Fargo prompted, "Suppose you tell me so we'll both know?"

"You're pokin' fun," Sam said. "But that's all right. I should humor you, this being your second-to-last day on earth, and all."

"I'm waiting," Fargo said.

"You're a hired killer, mister. You rent out your gun for money. The women hired you because they know they can't beat us without help." Sam smiled. "Darned clever of my pa, wouldn't you say?"

"Darned clever," Fargo said, "but not true. I'm only passing through. Ask the women. They'll tell you."

"Save it for the elders. They'll hear the case against you and decide on your fate."

After that Sam would not say a word although Fargo tried several times to present his side of events. Soon he had something else to preoccupy him. A pain spiked his chest and would not relent no matter how many times he shifted position.

Then, crossing a rise, Fargo looked back and saw the silhouette of a rider against the backdrop of bright blue sky. The killer was shadowing them. He opened his mouth to tell Sam but closed it again. The killer had disappeared. Sam would think he was making it up.

Toward the middle of the afternoon Bramwell called a halt. Fargo was slung off the Ovaro like a sack of flour and dragged to a log. He scraped an elbow and both shins, and when he sat up, tasted bits of grass in his mouth.

"Was that necessary?" Clover demanded of Bramwell and the man who had helped him.

"No, but it made me feel good," was Bramwell's sarcastic reply. He sat on the log, opened a saddlebag he had brought, and passed out jerky to his son and friends.

"What about us?" Clover asked.

"You both can starve for all I care." Bramwell bit off a piece and chomped with vigor. "I don't care if you are kin. By takin' up with that shrew, all the blood that's been spilled is on your head as well as hers."

"I haven't killed anyone, cousin."

"Maybe you haven't. But you've done something worse. You turned your back on your own family. You chose an outsider over your own. There are sins, and then there are sins, and that's the worst of any."

Fargo felt compelled to speak in her defense. "You can't blame her for doing what she thinks is right."

"Sure I can," Bramwell said, "especially when it costs the lives of those nearest and dearest to me." He grabbed Fargo by the front of the shirt. "I don't expect you to understand, but for us the clan is *everything*. We're born to it, we live for it, we die in it. Nothin' else matters. Nothin' at all." He shoved Fargo, hard. "The last time this much Jackson blood was spilled was twenty years ago, back in North Carolina before we packed up and came here. We had been feudin' with the Harker clan for pretty near a century. Then one day we caught the head of their clan alone in the woods and held him in chains until his kin agreed to our terms." Bramwell bit off more jerky. "We haven't lost a Jackson since, except by natural causes."

Sam wore a glum expression. "I wish there was some other way to deal with cousin Clover, Pa."

"You *still* feel sorry for her, boy? After Jesse was shot dead right in front of your eyes?" Bramwell shook the jerky at him. "You're a severe disappointment to me at times, Samuel. You think with your heart instead of your brain, just like your ma. That's what I get for lettin' her baby you when you were little. She was always makin' excuses for you, you being the youngest and all."

"Please don't start," Sam said.

"Afraid of the truth?" Bramwell asked. "You should know by now that I speak my mind, come what may."

Bowing his head, Sam walked off to be by himself.

Clover watched him with sorrow in her eyes. "You're a cruel man, Bramwell Jackson. That boy idolizes you and you treat him like pig droppin's."

"And you're a hypocrite, cousin Clover. If you cared half as much as you pretend to about any of us, you wouldn't have betrayed our trust." Bramwell took a last bite and stood. "This jabber serves no purpose. Mount up."

Once again Fargo was treated to the indignity of being slung over his horse. He willed his body to go limp so it would not be as uncomfortable and wondered what sort of reception awaited them in Jacksonville. As he hung there, head dangling, he happened to glance into the trees and his breath caught in his throat.

Dressed all in black, astride a black bay, the killer wasn't more than fifty yards away, brazenly watching everything that went on.

Fargo opened his mouth to tell the others but the killer reined into high brush and was gone. From the way the rider sat the bay, Fargo would swear it was a woman. He didn't have a good look at the rider's face and he couldn't say for certain that the rider had breasts, but judging by the rider's profile and posture and how the rider handled the reins, Fargo would bet every penny he had that he was right.

And he could think of only one woman it might be.

8

This time it was a shed. A smelly, moldy tool shed with cracks in the roof, a pile of dirty rags in one corner, and an assortment of tools, some badly rusted. Space had been cleared in the center and a stool placed there for Fargo to sit on. Then they had shackled his wrists and ankles with chains.

Fargo wasn't given food, he wasn't given water. They left him to endure the heat of the afternoon, saying as they went out that his trial would begin the next morning promptly at nine a.m.

The last he saw of Clover, she was being hauled into the general store.

Now, hunkered on the stool, the chains rattling with every movement he made, no matter how slight, Fargo peered through an inch-wide gap in the front door at the two Jacksons chosen to guard him. One had to be in his fifties, the other not much younger. Both were burly and scruffy and armed with rifles and long knives. The older one had the keys to the shackles dangling by a metal ring from his belt.

How to get those keys, that was the question burning in Fargo's brain. Somehow, some way, he must prevent them from stretching his neck. To that end, removing the shackles was essential.

His guards were talking. "It's a cryin' shame about

Jesse," the older one said. "Whoever did him in should be skinned alive."

"Bramwell thinks it was the Meriwether woman," the other observed. "May she rot in hell for all eternity. We should lay siege to the farm, Asher. Those females won't hold out for long without food and water."

"It might interest you to know, Seth, that Porter has cooked up a plan to end this nonsense once and for all. He says we have to do it quickly, before they bring in more hired guns like this fella in the shed."

"He claims he's no such thing."

"Wouldn't you if it was your life at stake?" Asher asked.

Tools were stacked against the left wall: a shovel, a hoe, several rakes, a pick, and a sledgehammer. None were of any use to Fargo. The sledge might shatter the leg chains but the noise would bring the guards. Hanging from nails on the right wall were a hammer, a pair of pruning shears, a scythe, a coil of rope, and several trowels. None of them did him any good, either. What Fargo needed most was something to pick the locks with.

Seth cradled his rifle in his brawny arms. "I'm lookin' forward to stringin' this gent up. The smart thing to do was hang someone long ago to show the women we mean business."

"We couldn't very well string up one of our own," Asher said.

"We can if they've killed kin," Seth disagreed. "And we'd only have to do it once. Stretchin' a neck would bring the others around, sure as shootin'."

There was more but Fargo didn't listen. He had spotted a small file on the floor under a bench. Only part of it was visible but it appeared to be thin enough to insert into the keyhole on the shackles. Maybe, just maybe, with a little jimmying it would do the job.

Holding the chains so they would rattle as little as

possible, Fargo eased off the stool. He slid one foot as far as the chain allowed, then did the same with the other. Stooping, he palmed the file and discovered it was broken. The piece he had was only four inches long. One end tapered to a thin point that was ideal for his purpose.

Returning to the stool, Fargo slowly sank down. None too soon.

The door was yanked wide open and Asher ducked his grizzled head inside. "Thought I heard a noise," he said suspiciously, eyeing the shackles and the four walls.

"I'm still here," Fargo said. Beyond Asher the western horizon was ablaze with vivid hues of pink, orange, and yellow. The sun was setting.

"If you have a notion of leavin' us, you can forget it," Asher said. "We're under orders to shoot if you set so much as your little toe outside this shed."

"I'm not a hired killer."

"Tell it to the elders tomorrow. Your fate is in their hands, not mine." Asher leaned further in. "If it were up to me, I'd blow out your wick where you sit. Jesse was my sister's son, and never a finer boy drew breath."

"I had nothing to do with his death," Fargo said, well aware it would go in one ear and out the other.

"So you keep sayin', mister. But killin' and lyin' go hand in hand, so don't be offended if I don't believe you." Snickering, Asher backed out and shut the door.

Fargo didn't waste a second. Reversing his grip on the broken file, he twisted his right wrist so he could insert it into the keyhole to the shackle on his left wrist. It slid in easily enough but when he turned it, nothing happened. He jiggled it back and forth and up and down, jiggled it until his fingers were sore and raw, but the shackle wouldn't open.

Night fell. The shed was mired in murk. Jacksonville might as well be a cemetery, it lay so quiet and still

63

under the stars. Then chains rattled outside the shed and footsteps shuffled near and Asher exclaimed, "What do we have here?"

"Porter says I'm to feed him."

Fargo recognized the voice and put his right eye to a crack. Clover's ankles were shackled but her arms were free and she was holding a large pot in one hand and a plate and spoon in the other.

"He can starve for all I care," Asher said. "It would serve him right for the misery he's caused."

"Then you go tell that to Porter," Clover said defiantly.

Asher muttered something, then turned and opened the shed door. "All right. In you go. But I'm keepin' the door open."

"Worried I'll try to run off, Uncle?" Clover hobbled inside, squatted, and set the pot on the ground. "Are you hungry?" She did not wait for an answer but removed the lid and began ladling a heaping portion of beans onto the tin plate. "I made these myself."

Fargo accepted the plate and the spoon. "I'm obliged."

"They have me doing all kinds of chores. Cookin', cleanin', mendin', you name it. The work has piled up with most of the women gone."

Considering that Fargo had not eaten in over a day, he was famished. The beans were delicious, and he commented as much.

"Thank you." Clover's teeth flashed white in the gloom. "My secret ingredient is five spoonfuls of brown sugar." She glanced over her shoulder, then bent forward. "You have to get out of here. I don't know how, but if you don't, you're as good as dead. The word is that Porter plans to make an example of you."

"What about innocent until proven guilty?" Fargo asked with his mouth full.

"Here it's guilty until proven innocent. They're al-

64

ready talkin' about how they plan to hang you from the old oak at the north end of town. Porter had someone go around lookin' for a suitable rope. He wanted a new one so it won't break when they slap your horse out from under you."

Any sympathy Fargo felt for the men of Jacksonville was fading. Meriwether had been wrong to turn the women against them, but now the men were about to do far worse. "Will Porter give me a chance to explain myself?"

"I can't rightly say. Even if he does, it won't count for much." Clover added more beans to his plate. "He's changed, Porter has. He was always so kind and considerate but now he's bitter and vengeful."

"If I get free, where will I find you?"

Clover shook her head. "Forget about me. It's sweet, but it will only get you killed. They keep me under guard in a back room of the general store when I'm not workin'."

Suddenly Asher thrust his head inside. "What's all the talkin'? And why is it takin' so long? He's got his food, girl. You can leave."

"I was told to wait and take the plate and spoon back with me," Clover said. "Give him a minute and he'll be done." When Asher grunted and turned away, she grinned and whispered, "I fibbed about takin' the stuff back. I'm just not in a hurry to scrub more floors."

"Did you say there are women still in town?" Fargo asked.

"Sure. Only about half joined the rebellion, as Porter is callin' it. The rest didn't see the wrong in Elly marryin' Billy and never believed that Porter would kill his own kinfolk." Clover's shoulders slumped. "I wish I had listened to them instead of Argent. If I had, you wouldn't be in this fix."

Fargo touched the tip of her chin. "You did what you felt you had to."

"I know, I know. Hindsight is always best. But I'm worried. Porter's patience has run out, and he's contemplatin' drastic measures. Measures that will bury a lot more of us."

"Where's my horse?" Fargo thought to ask.

"At the hitch rail in front of the tavern. But don't worry. Sam is takin' real good care of it. He's fed and watered it. And put your effects in the store, by the front counter."

"Thank him for me."

"Oh, he's not doing it out of the goodness of his heart," Clover said. "He's taken a shine to your pinto, and Bramwell has given his permission for the boy to have it after you've been hung." She placed a hand on his knee and lowered her voice even more. "If I can, I hope to slip out later tonight and set you free."

"How, without the key?" Fargo didn't want her harmed on his account.

"I'll think of something," Clover said, but she wasn't exactly brimming with confidence. Reaching up, she tugged on his beard. "Never give up hope."

Fargo didn't intend to. He was about to ask about his Henry when Asher filled the doorway.

"I don't like all this whisperin'. Time's up, whether he's done or not. Leave the plate and the spoon and skedaddle."

"As you wish, Uncle." Clover angrily slammed the lid to the pot and rose.

Winking at Fargo, she shut the door behind her.

Fargo admired her sand. He took his time eating the rest of the beans, and when he was done, tapped on the door and had Asher take the utensils so he wouldn't be interrupted later. Then he resumed his assault on the shackles. Minute after minute, for more than an hour and a half, he pried and twisted but the shackles refused to open.

The file just wasn't working. Fargo scanned the shed again, seeking something else. But it was now so dark he could barely see. His gaze fell on the bench and a jumbled pile of odds and ends: nails, pieces of wood, a screwdriver and pliers. Holding his wrist chains, he carefully moved to the bench for a better look.

Nothing was suitable. Fargo was turning back when a bucket of nails to the right of the bench caught his eye. Small, thin nails, the kind used on trim in a house. He chose one at random and returned to the stool.

Asher and Seth had moved a dozen feet away and Asher was lighting a corncob pipe. They were talking about the weather, and how they wished it would rain to help their crops.

Inserting the nail into the keyhole, Fargo hoped against hope. Once again the minutes dragged by on turtle's feet. Once again it proved unavailing. He had been at it over an hour and was about to give up when in frustration he jammed the nail in as far as it would go and when it met resistance he pushed harder. There was a *click* and the shackle parted.

Fargo stared in pleased surprise, then applied the nail to the shackle on his other wrist. One arm free was not enough. He needed both. But although he worked at the second shackle for twice as long as he had the first, it defied every effort.

Disgusted, Fargo sat with his chin in his hands and debated what he should do next. Outside, Seth had curled up on the ground with his rifle between his legs and his cheek resting on his hands.

"I'll wake you about two to spell me," Asher said.

Fargo stifled a yawn. He was tired enough to sleep for a week but if he didn't get the shackles off, his next rest would be permanent. He tried the nail again. He tried the file. He tried a metal spike. And all the while his eyelids grew heavier and heavier, until by two, when Asher roused Seth to relieve him, they were as heavy as horseshoes. Again and again he nearly dozed off. Again and again he snapped them open. Exhaustion claimed him about three. He dreamt

he was crossing the plains and encountered a number-
less herd of buffalo. He needed to eat, so he snuck
through the tall grass to get within rifle range when
without warning a strange sound caused the herd to
start in alarm and stampede to the south.

Fargo opened his eyes. He had slid off the stool
and was on his back on the ground. Something had
awakened him but he could not say what. He strained
his ears but heard nothing out of the ordinary. Slowly
sitting up, he noticed that the top and bottom edges
of the door were lighter than they should be. Puzzled,
he peered out and was appalled to find he had slept
most of the night away. The first rays of the new day
were erasing stars from the eastern sky.

Fargo shifted to climb back onto the stool before
his guards came to fetch him and felt a hard object
under his right palm. He held it up to see it better
and could not quite credit his eyesight. It was a key.
The key he needed to remove the shackles. Inserting
it, he twisted, and the shackle on his right wrist fell
to the dirt with a *clank* . . .

Fargo leaped to the conclusion the key had fallen
from Asher's belt during Clover's visit, and Asher
never noticed it was missing. He raised his face to the
crack in the door, and the hair at the nape of his
neck prickled.

Seth was on his back, a halo of scarlet framing his
head and shoulders. His throat had been slit from ear
to ear, the cut so deep, it was clean to the spine.

Asher had a knife buried to the hilt in the socket
of his right eye. His arms were out flung, his face
contorted in the fleeting horror that overcame him in
the few seconds between being stabbed and dying.

Someone had killed them, taken the key, and
dropped it inside the shed. "Clover?" Fargo whispered. There was no answer, but he could not think
of anyone else who would do it.

Confused and wary, Fargo hurriedly removed the

shackles around his ankles and emerged into the brisk breeze of impending dawn. It had occurred to him that if Clover had slain the guards, she would have entered the shed and helped free him. So it must be someone else. *But who?* he wondered. *And why?*

Fargo could not say what made him glance to his right. A stone's throw from town were dark woods. But not so dark he couldn't see the big black horse, and on it, wrapped in the folds of a long black slicker and wearing a broad-brimmed black hat, was the terror of the Ozarks.

9

Fargo glanced down, searching for a rifle, but neither Asher's nor Seth's were anywhere to be seen. Their knives were gone, too. He looked up, and the rider in black waved. The suggestion of a smile or a smirk curled the rider's mouth, then he wheeled the bay and melted into the forest.

What was that all about? Fargo wondered. He was turning to go when the answer hit him like a slap in the face. Jolted, he stared at the bodies. As surely as he was standing there, they had been slain by the rider in black. Which meant it was the killer who placed the key in the shed. The killer *wanted* him free. But why? To what end?

The crowing of a rooster brought Fargo's musing to an end. The sun would rise soon, and the good citizens of Jacksonville would be astir. He ran between two buildings to the street. Once he was sure it was deserted, he sprinted to the general store, hugging the shadows so early risers would be less apt to spot him.

The Ovaro was dozing at the hitch rail near the tavern. It heard him, and as he went by it nickered a greeting. Hoping no one had heard, Fargo came to the general store and stopped at the storefront window. No one was in sight. Clover had mentioned she was in a room at the back. There was a narrow hall to the right of the counter, but a curtain had been hung across it.

Ducking low, Fargo darted to the front door and gingerly tried the latch. The door wasn't locked. Opening it wide enough to slip his right arm in, he groped above his head. Some stores had tiny bells over their doors so the proprietor knew when customers came and went. He ran his fingers the width of the jamb but did not find one.

Slipping inside, Fargo eased the door shut and stalked to the counter. His saddle and other possessions were right where Clover had said they would be. Eagerly sliding the Henry out, he levered a round into the chamber.

Somewhere someone coughed. Fargo turned to stone just as the partition parted and a hefty man in overalls and suspenders ambled out, wearily rubbing his bloodshot eyes. "I'm hungry, too," he said over a shoulder. "As soon as they get here, I'm going home to have breakfast." Fargo hunkered below the counter, only his eyes showing.

The guard walked to a shelf lined with jars of honey popcorn balls, gumdrops, and other hard candy, opened one, and helped himself to a piece of peanut brittle. "Do you want some?" he hollered.

"Taffy would be nice," came the reply. "Or some of that fudge Mabel makes. I'll be right there."

The crowing of the rooster reminded Fargo he did not have much time. Hill folk were early risers. Someone might show up at any moment.

Again the partition parted and out stepped a scrawny specimen toting a shotgun. "I've always had a sweet tooth. When I was knee-high to a calf, I'd lick my finger and dip it in the brown sugar and Ma would throw a hissy fit."

Fargo glided toward them.

Now both were at the shelf, and the man with the

sweet tooth was taking a thick piece of fudge from a large container. "This is from last week's batch. It's hard as a rock." That did not stop him from stuffing half into his mouth. "Mabel better make some more soon."

They turned, and Fargo chose that moment to unfurl and point the Henry. "Easy or hard, it's your choice."

Dumbfounded, the pair gawked.

"No one has to die," Fargo stressed to forestall a rash act. "All I want is the woman. Put your rifles down and your hands behind your backs." As he spoke, he moved closer. He was only several feet from them when the scrawny one blurted, "Like hell!" and jerked the shotgun up.

Fargo was on them before the man could fire. He rammed the Henry's muzzle into the scrawny one's gut, and when the man doubled over, brought the stock crashing down on the top of his head. That left the peanut brittle lover, who had hold of his rifle by the barrel and swung it like a club. Ducking, Fargo planted his left boot on the other's instep, and when the man yipped and hiked his leg in reflex, Fargo stretched him out like a limp rag.

Once more the rooster crowed.

Dashing to the partition, Fargo flung it aside. Two doors were on the right, one on the left. He tried the nearest and there she was, over in a corner, her arms and legs in chains, as his had been.

"Skye!" Clover cried.

Fargo hastened to her side and inserted the key into one of her shackles. The key worked. In moments he had her free.

"A key?" Clover said quizzically. "Where in the world did you get that?"

Pulling her to her feet, Fargo replied, "We'll talk later." Keeping hold of her forearm, he ran toward the front of the store. He thought he had heard a sound and worried that one of the men he had slugged was still conscious. Shoving past the partition, he saw them sprawled where he had left them.

Clover shifted toward the front and blurted, "No! Not now!"

Someone else had arrived and stood just inside the front door. An older man, in his seventies if he was a day, his gray beard neatly trimmed, his attire consisting of a jacket, white shirt, and pants. A straw hat was pulled low over his beetling brows.

Fargo remembered seeing him before, that first day in Jacksonville, sharing a plug of tobacco with Bramwell. He pointed the Henry. "Out of our way."

Amazingly, the man stood his ground. He calmly regarded the pair on the floor, and equally calmly regarded Fargo and Clover. "Well, well. This is a surprise. How on earth did the two of you get loose?"

"Didn't you hear me?" Fargo demanded.

The man drew himself up to his full height. "Do you have any notion who I am, outsider?"

Until that instant Fargo hadn't. Belatedly, he saw how strongly the man resembled Bramwell—the same eyes, the same big hands, the same build. "You're Porter Jackson, the head of the clan."

Porter smiled and nodded. "I advise you to surrender. Or need I bring up that your life is in my hands? All I need do is give the word and you and the rebel will be snuffed out like candles."

"What are you—" Fargo began, and then saw that the street was filled with people. Twenty to thirty, most of them men, including Bramwell, but a few women and children, as well. They were staring at the general store, waiting for their leader to reappear.

"You can't get away," Porter said smugly. "Even if you reach your horse, you will be shot dead before you climb on." He extended his right hand. "For your own sakes, give me your rifle. I give you my word your trial will be as fair as possible, and when we hang you, it will be quick and painless."

Fargo could not help chuckling in amusement. "I didn't live as long as I have by being stupid."

Porter's face and tone became harsh. "Must you compound your evil? Haven't you done enough?"

"I haven't done *anything*," Fargo snapped, anger washing through him like bitter bile. "And I'm not telling you again." He centered a bead on Porter's chest. "Move or die." He was bluffing. It went against his grain to gun down an unarmed man, even one this misguided.

The patriarch glared his refusal. Then Bramwell shouted his name, and Porter's anger was replaced by a devious grin.

"Pa? What's takin' so long? Have them bring her out so we can get this over with."

Before Fargo could think to stop him, Porter cupped his hands to his mouth. "They're free, son! Both of them! And they have a gun on me!"

A roar of inarticulate rage from Bramwell was the catalyst for eight or nine men to rush the general store. Swiveling, Fargo banged off two shots through the front window, aiming high so none of the women or children would be hit. The hill folk thought they were being fired at, and scattered. One man shot back, the slug imbedding itself in the ceiling, but stopped shooting at an angry yell from Bramwell.

"Quit firin', you idiot! My pa is in there!"

Porter made no attempt to run. Leisurely folding his arms, he smiled and asked, "Now what, outsider? They'll surround the store. You'll never get out alive."

Striding over, Fargo gripped him by the scruff of his shirt and shoved him toward the counter. "They won't try anything so long as I have you."

"Think so?" Porter responded, and threw back his head. "Bramwell? Orville? Do you hear me? You're to rush in and kill the stranger! Now! Right this instant!"

Fargo swung toward the door but the street remained empty.

"Didn't you hear me?" Porter shouted.

Glowering faces jutted from corners and peered through windows across the street. Bramwell appeared, a bulge under his shirt where a new bandage had been applied. "We hear you, Pa! But we won't risk you being killed!"

"Damn him," Porter fumed. "When this is over, I'm taking a hickory switch to his backside."

"He's a little old for a spanking," Fargo mentioned, his eyes on Bramwell, who was gesturing to someone he couldn't see.

"No son or daughter is ever too old," Porter said. "Spare the rod and spoil the child. That's always been my view. And no one can accuse me of spoilin' mine."

A shadow flitted across the far end of the front window. Fargo caught sight of a swarthy bearded face and the dull glint of a revolver. He fired at the same split second as the would-be assassin, and the bearded face dissolved in a crimson spray. The man's death wail rose loud to the sky, and he pitched to the dirt, his frame racked by violent convulsions.

"Matthew!" Porter cried, and started toward the door.

Fargo reached Porter just as he reached the threshold. Seizing hold of the back of Porter's jacket, Fargo pushed him to one side. The clan patriarch collided with a rack of dry goods and both crashed to the floor.

A shot rang out. Lead smacked into the jamb a handsbreadth from Fargo's head, and he crouched behind the nearest cover: the pickle barrel.

"Damn you!" Porter raged. "That was my second oldest son you just killed!"

"He was trying to kill me."

Porter threw a bolt of cloth off his legs and shook

a fist in seething fury. "I'll see you suffer! I'll see you on your knees beggin' for your life! You'll know the torment of the damned before I'm through!" Trembling with rage, he rose and charged, his fingers hooked like claws. The man was practically beside himself.

Fargo did not dare stand up. He would expose himself to the hillmen outside, who would cut him down without a second's hesitation. If he was still alive, Porter would pounce and keep him there long enough for the others to rush in.

"Make you suffer!" Porter railed. He had only a few steps to go.

Fargo dropped and rolled. Not away from the patriarch, toward him. His idea was to bowl Porter over and subdue him but Porter was far more nimble than he reckoned. Leaping into the air, Porter sailed right over him.

Stopping, Fargo surged onto one knee. He expected Porter to come at him again, and cocked his arms to swing the Henry. But Porter Jackson was bolting for the door, and the street. Fargo had no hope of reaching him before he made it out, and in desperation he did the only thing he could; he seized a bolt of burgundy cloth and threw it at Porter's legs. It caught Porter across the ankles and down Porter crashed, crying out in pain.

"Pa!" Bramwell shouted. "Are you all right?"

Porter was scrabbling for the doorway, his left leg not moving as it should, his teeth grit in determination.

Fargo reached him first. Hooking an arm under the patriarch's, he executed a hip toss that sent Porter tottering against a shelf. Merchandise toppled, and out in the street several guns blasted in a spontaneous volley. Diving flat, Fargo heard lead *thwack* into the walls.

A bellow from Bramwell ended the gunfire. "Stop

shootin', damn you! Or so help me, I'll kill the next man who does!" He paused. "Pa, did any of those shots hit you? Are you hurt?"

"I'm fine," Porter shouted, "except for a son who doesn't mind his betters."

"Keepin' you alive is all that matters to me," Bramwell said. "Hold it against me if you want, but I'd do it the same all over again."

Fargo slammed the door and twisted. Clover was hunkered by the candy, untouched. Porter was holding on to a shelf with one arm and holding his left leg with the other. "You'll get yourself killed if you keep that up," Fargo said.

"My life means nothin', outsider," Porter snarled. "It's the clan that counts, and only the clan. Which is why I will do whatever I must to end the killin'." He straightened, but not without effort, and when he put his weight on his left foot, his leg almost buckled.

"Is it broken?" Clover asked.

"What do you care?" Porter retorted. "You made it clear where your loyalties lie, girl, when you sided with that uppity teacher against your own flesh and blood. You and the other rebels have done more to harm our family than all the enemies we've ever had combined."

"I did what I thought was right," Clover protested.

Porter Jackson's lips were a thin, vicious slash of resentment. "Have you forgotten what you were taught? Didn't your folks tell you that the clan is *always* in the right, no matter what?"

"Even when the clan is wrong?"

An incarnation of wrath, Porter limped toward her, extending a rigid finger as if it were a cane. "Who are *you* to pass judgment on *us*? For hundreds of years the Jacksons have always been there for each other. It's us against the rest of the world, and we never, *ever,* turn on one another."

Clover rose and balled her fists. "What about Elly

and Billy, found murdered with your knife close by? What about—" She suddenly gave a start and glanced sharply toward the front door.

Fargo spun on the balls of his boots, pumping the Henry's lever as he turned. He had been careless. He had let them distract him. And now Bramwell Jackson had crossed the street and was reaching for the latch.

10

The instant Fargo turned, Bramwell Jackson raised his arms into the air and shouted, "Don't shoot! All I want is to talk! I'm unarmed!"

Sure enough, Bramwell's holster was empty and he was not carrying a rifle. Suspicious of a trick, Fargo sidled into the shadows. "You can come in. But keep your hands where I can see them." To Porter he said, "Stay right where you are."

Bramwell blinked a few times, until his eyes adjusted to the dim interior. He saw his father. "Pa! Why are you standin' like that? Have they hurt you?"

"Sprained my ankle, is all," the father answered. "What are you doing in here? Go back out and give the order to riddle this place. I want these two dead."

"I can't do that, Pa. You might be hit." Bramwell could not keep the concern out of his voice.

"You're refusin' to do as I tell you?" Porter's jaw muscles twitched and he hobbled a step toward his son and might have taken another but he stopped when Fargo shifted the Henry in his direction. "Have you forgotten who I am?"

"You're my pa—" Bramwell began.

"And you're to honor your father and mother and do as they say. Isn't that what the Good Book teaches?" Porter said. "But I'm also more than that. I'm the head of our clan. I'm to be obeyed without question. It's how the Jacksons have done things for more generations than there are leaves on trees. So don't shame me, boy. Go relay my instructions to the others."

"I can't, Pa," Bramwell said. "You're too important to risk losin'. And that's not just me talkin'. The rest of the elders don't want you to come to harm, either."

"They told you that?" Porter sounded surprised.

"Jacob and Isaiah and the others are over at the feed store. They put it to a vote, and I'm to do whatever it takes to get you out alive. With your cooperation, or not." Bramwell faced Fargo. "So here's what I'm proposin'. Let my pa go, and Clover and you can ride out free as jays."

"Just like that?" Fargo was skeptical. "What's to stop you from shooting us in the back?"

"You have our word," Bramwell said.

Fargo was blunt. "It's not enough."

"You don't understand." Bramwell gestured at Porter. "We'll do whatever it takes. He means that much to us."

"To you, maybe." But Fargo had seen for himself that some clan members did not feel the same.

"There has to be a way we can work this out," Bramwell insisted. "What if we all leave town? Every last one of us? And I saddle your horse and bring it right up to the door? Just tell us what you want us to do and by God we'll do it."

Fargo liked the idea of having the Ovaro saddled, and said so.

Bramwell immediately went to the counter, slung Fargo's saddle over his good shoulder, and with the saddle blanket in his other hand, hastened out.

Porter's jaw muscles had started twitching again. "I never thought I'd live to see the day when the fruit of my loins would show yellow. I should beat him until his hide won't hold shucks."

"But he's doing it to save you," Clover said.

"Did I ask him to, little missy?" Porter sneered. "No. To the contrary. I'd as soon blow my own brains out as let you escape. The other elders should know better but I reckon the whole lot of them ain't got the sense God gave geese."

"Why, Porter Jackson. You're nothin' but a mean, bitter, headstrong old man who always has to be right, and to hell with everyone else." Clover's dander was up. "This whole awful mess is on your shoulders. If you had been more understandin', if you had listened to reason instead of insistin' everyone bow to your will, none of this would have happened."

"How dare you!"

A full-fledged argument flared but Fargo had more important considerations. He moved closer to the window so he could see down the street to the hitch rail. The Ovaro shied when Bramwell tried to throw the saddle blanket on but quieted when Bramwell spoke softly and made it a point to move slowly. The pinto twisted its head to watch the proceedings. Bramwell cinched the saddle and took the reins to lead it over, but the Ovaro balked, stamping a heavy hoof.

Bramwell glanced at the store as if to say, "I'm trying," then gently pulled on the reins while coaxing the Ovaro along. Reluctantly, the great stallion let him lead it under the overhang within a few feet of the door. Then, letting the reins dangle, Bramwell came back in, smiling broadly.

"We're all set! I've kept my end of the bargain. Now you keep yours and let my pa go."

"Not so fast," Fargo said, scanning the street. Scores of unfriendly faces peered out windows and around corners. "You said something about emptying the settlement."

"Give us fifteen minutes," Bramwell said, and rotated.

"One thing," Fargo trained the Henry on Porter. "I'll have my rifle on your father every foot of the way—"

Bramwell held up his right hand. "I know, I know. No need to say more. I give you my word no one will try to stop you." He smiled at his father, received a scowl of parental disapproval in return, and briskly exited.

"See? He completely ignored my wishes," Porter grumbled. "Tryin' to talk sense into that boy is like tryin' to scratch your ear with your elbow."

"He's a grown man," Clover observed.

Porter's dark eyes narrowed to slits. "No matter how old he gets, I'll always be older. No matter how much experience he has, I'll always have more. There was a time when those your age looked up to their elders and always did as they were told."

Another argument ensued. Fargo sidestepped to the right until he could survey both ends of the street without being seen. Bramwell and a bunch of older men were by the feed store, talking. A white-haired man with a beard down past his belt appeared to be in charge, and when he nodded and motioned, the rest fanned out and began yelling for everyone to clear out of Jacksonville.

So far, so good, Fargo thought. But he had no way of verifying they all left as promised. It could be a trap. Some might lie low, waiting for him to appear so they could buck him out in a blaze of lead. He glanced at the Ovaro, patiently waiting with its head low, and thought of an oversight on his part. Why ride double when there was no need? Keeping low, he moved to the door and opened it partway. "Bramwell!"

Out in the middle of the street, Bramwell was hustling his kin along. "What is it?" he shouted. "I'm doing as you wanted, aren't I?"

"I need a horse for your cousin. A good horse," Fargo stressed. "Saddled and next to mine."

"Is that all?" Bramwell barked orders at a pair of younger men, who dashed off. "Anything else? Food? Water? Ammunition?"

Fargo shook his head. There was plenty in the store. And that reminded him. He walked to a rifle case and took down a Sharps. One of his favorite rifles, he had used a Sharps for years before switching to the Henry. But it was too big and too heavy for Clover, he decided. He chose a smaller, lighter English-made model seldom seen on the frontier because the cartridges had a tendency to jam. "Can you shoot?" he asked.

"Are you kiddin'?" Clover chuckled. "I was a tomboy once. I could outride, outrun, and outshoot half the boys around." She accepted it and hefted it, then jammed the stock to her shoulder. "I once dropped a duck on the wing at sixty yards."

Drawers under the gun case contained ammunition. Fargo selected the right box and handed it to her. "Help yourself to whatever else you need."

He needed a revolver. The pistol case contained mostly used models, including a Colt with dozens of nicks and scrapes. It was the same caliber as his and would suffice until he reclaimed his own.

"Look at you two!" Porter snorted. "Common robbers as well as horse thieves and killers. There's just no end to your evil, is there?"

"I'll see that the horse is returned," Fargo promised, and fished in a pocket for money. "Everything else will be paid for."

"Payin' for something you steal is like shuttin' the barn door after the mules get out. It don't hardly make the stealin' right," Porter pontificated.

The man was as tactless as a drunk Kiowa. Fargo went to the window to check on the exodus. Men, women, and children, singly and in groups, were filing south. Most glared at the store window as they went by. Which was why he stayed in the shadows. The temptation might be more than some could resist.

Porter would not shut up. "Even if you get away, you're only buyin' yourselves time. Eventually we will hunt you down."

Clover approached him. "What if I convinced Argent Meriwether to sit down with you and hash things out?"

"I'd split her skull with an axe," Porter answered. "That female has done more to tear our clan apart than all the feuds we ever fought back in North Carolina and the Old Country combined."

Fargo tore his gaze from the procession. "What about the women who are with her? Your own kin? Would you split their skulls, too?"

"Were it up to me I'd banish the whole lot," Porter said, "but the rest of the elders aren't as sensible as I am. They'd likely vote to punish them but leave the punishin' to me." Porter's wrinkled face became a mirror of fierce glee. "That's why bullwhips were invented."

"You would whip women and children?" Fargo was growing to loathe the man more by the minute.

Porter laughed. "You make it sound like punishin' wrongdoers is bad. But to answer your silly question, yes, yes, a hundred times yes! I'll whip the back of every rebel down to the bone and I won't have any regrets later." He laughed louder. "How's them apples?"

Fargo suppressed an urge to belt him in the mouth. Instead, he focused on the scene outside. A few stragglers were jogging to catch up with the rest of Jacksonville's citizenry. Soon only Bramwell remained. "Satisfied?" he called out.

Craning his neck both ways, Fargo ensured that every window, every doorway, every corner, was deserted. A clatter of hooves alerted him to a man riding a mare up the street. It was the horse they had chosen for Clover. The man dismounted, handed the reins to Bramwell, and departed on the heels of everyone else. Not wasting a second, Bramwell brought the mare over beside the Ovaro.

"Here you are! I've done everything you wanted! Let's get this over with!" His hands out from his sides, Bramwell smiled and backed away.

Fargo made bold to show himself. "Once you're gone we'll head north."

Bramwell tried to gaze into the store. "Hang on, Pa!" he yelled, breaking into a run. "We'll have you safe in no time!"

The rest of the hill folk were almost out of rifle range. Fargo waited until they were, then beckoned to Clover and Porter. She had a bulging burlap bag filled with coffee, food, and other supplies. Porter had helped himself to a broom and was using it as a crutch. Careful not to step from under the overhang, Fargo covered the patriarch while trying to watch his own back.

"May you rot in hell, the both of you," summed up Porter's view of the state of affairs.

Glistening dust particles hung suspended in the air. On the porch of a cabin farther down the street, a mongrel stirred, scratched itself, and lay back down, lazing in the morning sun. Otherwise, Jacksonville might as well have been a ghost town. No sounds broke the stillness.

Fargo was still not satisfied. A window on the second floor of the feed store was open, a yawning dark cavity that might conceal a lurking gunman. So was the door to the town tavern.

"Nerves actin' up, are they?" Porter taunted. "I can tell you're as nervous as a cat in a room full of hound dogs."

A feeling of unseen eyes on them grew. "Against the wall," Fargo directed, then relieved Clover of the

85

burlap bag so she could climb on the mare. It was heavier than he expected and he almost dropped it. "What the hell is in here?" he groused. "An anvil?"

"Extra ammunition and other stuff I reckoned we'd need," Clover revealed. Leaning down, she slung it across her saddle. "I'll tie it proper once we're in the clear." She moved her leg so it pressed against the bag, then transferred her rifle to her other hand and gripped the reins. "Ready when you are, handsome."

Fargo forked leather. The moment he took his eyes off Porter, the old man spun and hobbled off as fast as his sprained ankle allowed. "That's far enough," Fargo warned, thumbing back the Henry's hammer to accent his point.

Porter turned and grinned. "Can't blame a coon for tryin', can you? You would do the same if you were in my boots."

"Walk in front of us," Fargo said, wagging the Henry. That way, anyone will think twice before starting something. Or so he hoped.

With the bristle end of the broom propped under his arm, Porter limped north. He was in remarkably fine spirits, given the circumstances, and freely flapped his gums. "Yes, sir. I can't begin to say how tickled I'll be when the two of you are on the judgement seat. After you've been dealt with, we'll pay the Meriwether woman and Patrice a visit out at the farm and demand they tell us where Joseph got to."

Clover betrayed her surprise. "Joe is missin'? Patrice never said a word all the time I was out there."

"Mighty strange, don't you think?" Porter responded. "A wife not worryin' where her husband traipsed off to? Shows how much she truly cared, if you ask me."

"Joe wanted Elly to honor her promise to marry Billy, and that made Patrice mad," Clover explained for Fargo's benefit. "She was even madder when he sided with the elders against her."

"And then poor Joseph up and disappeared. Coincidence? I think not." Porter cackled as if it were the funniest thing ever. "Patrice claimed that the last she saw of him, he had packed a valise and was on his way into town to stay here until her temper cooled. But he never showed up."

Despite his best intentions, Fargo was paying more attention to them than he was to their surroundings. He remedied that by twisting in the saddle to confirm Bramwell and the rest of the hill folk were well to the south of the settlement, and then scanned the dust-streaked buildings on both sides of the narrow street. Porter was prattling on about something or other, and it occurred to him that the old man was talking much louder than was necessary. Too late, the most likely reason struck him like a bolt of lightning out of the ether, and he shifted to the right and then the left.

A bearded man with a rifle was at a nearby window, taking aim.

11

Only the fact that the Henry happened to be pointed in the general direction of the window saved Fargo. All he had to do was shift the barrel a few degrees and shoot. At the blast, the window shattered in a shower of gleaming shards and the man was flung backward as if slammed into by an invisible battering ram.

"What in the—" Clover cried. The rest of whatever she said was drowned out by the boom of a rifle behind them.

Another hillman had rounded a corner and was firing on the fly. But in his haste he was not taking aim.

Twisting, Fargo shot from the hip. His first round spun the man in his tracks, his second added a new nostril.

Shouts sounded from different quarters. More Jacksons appeared, some at windows, some in doorways, some from between buildings. It was a trap. Bramwell had tricked them to lure them out in the open. "Ride!" Fargo bawled at Clover, and gave her mare a hard slap on the rump that sent it galloping on ahead.

Porter Jackson was tittering like a lunatic while hopping up and down on his good leg and waving the broom as if it were a lance. "Kill him!" he screeched. "Kill the outsider, boys! Kill him dead, dead, dead!"

Fargo used his spurs on the stallion. Guns boomed

on all sides, and lead sizzled uncomfortably close to his ear. His hat was nearly plucked from his head. To free one hand for riding, he shoved the Henry into its scabbard and drew the Colt.

The next moment a burly hillman loomed directly in his path, holding a double-barreled shotgun.

Instantly, Fargo fired. The man's right eye burst in a grisly spray, and then the Ovaro was past and flying toward the north end of the street. But other enemies were waiting. Before he could reach the forest, he must run a bristling gauntlet of gun barrels.

Bending low, Fargo reined left and then right. Gun smoke billowed from several points, filling him with fear that the Ovaro would be hit. He spotted a man in a doorway and they fired simultaneously but it was the hillman who clutched at his throat and dropped. A rifle spanged from the mouth of an alley and Fargo responded in kind. He shot a man on a roof, shot another who foolishly rushed from the shadows swinging an axe.

Clover had reached the tree line and slowed to wait for him. "Keep going!" Fargo hollered, and emptied the last chamber in the Colt into the gray-flecked face of a Jackson with a squirrel gun.

A few more yards and Fargo was past the last of the buildings and crossing an open space. Rifles and pistols crackled like fireworks behind him. It was little short of a miracle that he and the pinto reached cover unscathed.

He had told Clover to keep going but she had gone only another ten yards and reined up. A horrendous risk on her part. Lead smacked into tree trunks and chipped slivers from branches and sent leaves flying. On top of that, riders were in pursuit.

Slowing as he drew abreast of her, Fargo gave the mare a harder slap, saying, "Are you trying to get yourself killed? *Ride,* damn it."

Ride they did. For an hour Fargo pushed their animals ever deeper into the verdant Ozarks, over rolling mountains and across lush dales. They rode until he was convinced beyond any shadow of doubt that they had eluded the hill folk. Eventually, with the Ovaro and the mare lathered with sweat and the mare wheezing heavily, unaccustomed as she was to so much exertion, Fargo came on a small spring nestled among overhanging woodland giants and flanked on one side by a boulder-strewn hill. It was here he halted.

Clover stiffly dismounted and pressed a hand to the small of her back. "I thought I was a good rider but you put me to shame. I'm sore in places I've never been sore before." She grinned. "I could use a back rub later."

"We'll see," Fargo said as he began stripping the pinto.

"Is something the matter? You look mad enough to kick a puppy."

"I am." Fargo was sick and tired of being played for a jackass. Sick and tired of people trying to kill him because they thought he was someone he wasn't. He had been accused of crimes he had not committed. He had been insulted and belittled and lied to. He had been poked, prodded, tied up, and chained. This last incident was the last straw. He was fed up. It was high time he showed the Jacksons that they didn't have the god-given right to ride roughshod over anyone they liked.

Porter and Bramwell had tricked him, and tricked him good. That whole business about Porter wanting to beat his son for giving in had been a sham. Porter knew the whole time that Bramwell would never let them leave Jacksonville alive. It had been a ploy from start to finish.

Fargo never intended to get involved in their little war. He had seen a woman held captive and freed her, and if she hadn't accidentally pushed him over that cliff and taken the Ovaro, he would have been long gone by now. But no. One misunderstanding had led to another, to where he had a whole settlement out to turn him into worm food and a mysterious rider in black who had outwitted him twice now, with nearly fatal consequences both times.

Enough was enough. For better or worse, whether he liked it or not, Fargo was involved. And he was not leaving until he settled accounts with all those who had wronged him.

"Are you sure you're all right?" Clover intruded on his somber thoughts. "You weren't wounded, were you?"

Fargo forced a smile. "I'm fine. Why don't you gather some firewood and I'll tend to the horses?"

"I get it," Clover said. "You want to be alone. Why didn't you just say so?" She flounced into the undergrowth muttering something about men.

As Fargo worked, he reviewed the sequence of events since he first saw her. He went over everything everyone had said, weeding out what was true and what might not be. He needed to sort it all out before he could decide how best to deal with those who had wronged him.

Clover returned with her arms laden with dead limbs, whistling merrily. "I've forgiven you," she said as she broke the limbs to make their fire. "I can't stay mad at someone who has saved my life so many times."

"Decent of you," Fargo said, plopping her saddle next to his own.

"I'm serious," Clover misunderstood. "I'm forever in your debt. Anything I can do for you, anything at all, you have but to ask."

Fargo contemplated the twin mounds outlined under her shirt. "Maybe later. Right now I want you to tell me about Patrice's farmhouse. How many rooms does it have?"

Clover stopped snapping limbs. "Whatever for?

Surely you're not thinkin' of going back there? Argent has probably given orders to have you shot on sight." But she did as he asked, and later, after they had spread out their blankets and were seated side by side, with the fire crackling and the tantalizing aroma of brewing coffee reminding Fargo of how hungry he was, Clover leaned against him and gave him the sultry look of a Denver dove.

"So what do you have percolatin' in that mind of yours?" she wondered. "Where do we go from here?"

"You're going somewhere safe," Fargo answered. "We'll meet up again after I'm done."

"We're splitting up?" Clover was hugely disappointed. "Why? I haven't been a burden, have I? And what do you mean by 'done'? Done what, exactly?"

Fargo gave her a piece of peanut brittle. "Here. Chew on this."

"Now I'm askin' too many questions, is that it?" Clover sat back, her spine as straight as a washboard. "Well, you sure have changed. One minute you can't keep your hands off me, the next you want to get rid of me."

The surest way to divert a woman's anger, Fargo had found, was to stimulate their unquenchable female curiosity. "Who do you think that rider in black is?"

"Him? I don't know."

"Why a 'him' and not a 'her'?" Fargo asked. "It could easily be a woman."

"I disagree," Clover said flatly. "None of them would kill their own relatives. Especially poor, sweet Harriet, who never harmed a soul in her life and never uttered a harsh word against anyone."

Fargo still believed her death had been an accident. "You don't know anyone who rides a big bay?"

After pondering, Clover shook her head.

"How about the teacher from Philadelphia?"

"Argent?" Clover laughed and slapped her leg.

"Why, she can't hardly climb on a horse without fallin' off. She's never ridden a day in her life."

"Then how did she get to Jacksonville?"

"My, you have a suspicious mind. For your information, Argent hired a man with a buggy to bring her. And since the school is near town, she always walked back and forth. Patrice has been givin' her lessons but she still can't ride worth a lick."

Fargo had a thought. "Patrice must be a good rider."

"What are you suggestin'? That she's out for revenge because of Elly? That she murdered Joe, her own husband, and has been on a killin' spree ever since?" Clover shook her head. "No. I can't see it. She loved Joe too much to do him in. And don't forget, women as well as men have been killed. It makes no kind of sense for Patrice to kill those on her side."

She had a point, Fargo conceded. Just as it made no sense for Porter to kill those on his side. But *someone* was sure as hell going around dispensing death. If he could figure out the reason, the culprit would not be hard to identify.

"Now suppose you tell me a little about yourself," Clover said. "Where you were born, what you do, the things you like most in this world."

"A glass of good whiskey and a friendly game of cards."

Clover waited, and when she saw that was all he was going to say, she responded, "That's it? There must be more to your life. Where are your kin? Where do you call home?"

Leaning back, Fargo nodded at the vault of trees and the oval of azure sky above the clearing. "You're looking at it."

"Huh?" Clover's forehead creased. "Oh. You wander where you please, livin' off the land? I envy you. We all have a secret hankerin' to see more of the world but few of us ever have the gumption to make our hankerin' real." She broke off a stem of grass and stuck it between her teeth as she had done before, an unconscious habit that was quite endearing. "Take me, for instance. When I was little, my head was filled with visions of England and Europe and places like that. You know, where ladies wear fancy dresses and spend their nights dancin' and courtin' and havin' the time of their lives."

Fargo opened his saddlebags to take out a lucifer and light their fire.

"Truth is," Clover said, "you're the most excitin' thing that's happened to me since who flung the chunk. I never have taken to my kin all that much. Not one of them has the imagination of a goat."

"Leave," Fargo said simply.

"Would that it were so easy," Clover sadly replied. "As much as they bore me, they're my kinfolk. Porter might think I'm pond scum but I'll never turn my back on my own. Or do them harm."

"Is there someone in your clan who would?"

"Honest answer? No. Oh, sure, there have been spats from time to time. But it's human nature to disagree. Until this terrible business started, all of us got along fairly well."

"No one has ever made threats? No one ever came to blows?" In a settlement the size of Jacksonville, Fargo figured it was only natural there would be a few hotheads.

"The last fight I can remember was nigh on eight or nine years ago," Clover related. "Two brothers, Barnaby and Melton, took to arguin' over a girl. But they made up afterwards."

"Have any other outsiders been through here recently besides me?" It was a long shot but Fargo had to explore every possibility.

"A patent medicine man came through the territory two months ago, but we don't cotton to his kind so he took his fake medicines elsewhere. Before that, a drummer sellin' ladies' shoes stopped in Jacksonville and couldn't understand why us women would rather spend what little money we have on things less frivolous." Clover snickered. "Who needs more than one pair of shoes every four or five years, anyhow?"

Fargo fished a handful of honey popcorn balls from the burlap bag and offered some to her. She took some and popped them one by one into her mouth.

"I could eat a whole bear right about now."

Flicking a popcorn ball into his own mouth, Fargo said, "I'll go hunting for supper later." Twilight was best. That was when deer were often abroad. Or he might come across a rabbit or squirrel.

"There's no rush. I can hold out." Clover stretched her leg to rub her foot against his. "Which gives us the whole afternoon to ourselves. Any idea how you would like to spend it?"

The invitation in her tone and hooded gaze brought to mind the magnificent swell of her bare breasts and the soft, silken texture of her inner thighs, and a stirring started below Fargo's belt. "Women," he said, and grinned.

"Am I being too forward? After last night, you have me cravin' more," Clover confessed. "You're the kind of gent most gals can't resist, and something tells me you know it."

Fargo surveyed the surrounding woods. They were quiet and peaceful. He would stake his bottom dollar it was safe for them to enjoy themselves, but he had been wrong before and he did not care to be caught with his pants down around his boots. The last time that happened, about six months ago, he had been lucky to live to pull them up again.

"Cat got your tongue?" Clover asked. "Most men would be plumb flattered by my compliment."

"I am," Fargo assured her.

"Oh, really?" Clover moved his saddlebags and slid

closer, her breasts jiggling under her shirt. Draping a slender arm across his broad shoulders, she traced the outer edge of his ear with a fingernail, and winked. "Talk is cheap hereabouts. If you're so all-fired grateful, why don't you prove it?"

Fargo grinned. "You want that back rub, is that it?"

"That, and a whole lot more."

12

Fargo pulled her to him and molded his mouth to hers. She tasted of peanut brittle and popcorn balls. Her velvet tongue swirled in a delicate dance with his, then rimmed his teeth. She was a great kisser. He sucked on her tongue while his hands were busy sculpting the contours of her back, from her slender shoulders to her shoulder blades to where her spine met her hips.

Clover, meanwhile, had removed his hat. The Colt was gouging her side so she unhitched his gun belt and removed that, too. Prying at his buckskin shirt, she slid a warm hand over his washboard abdomen to his chest. There she lingered, lightly running her fingers back and forth. "You have a hard body," she whispered in his ear. "Not flabby, like some. I like that."

Something else was hard and growing harder by the second. Fargo ran his fingers through her silken blond hair, sucked on her ear, and planted kisses along her chin. With his other hand he undid her shirt and soon gained access to her marvelous breasts, so delightfully shaped, their nipples taut and inviting. He kissed one and then the other, and she shivered.

"I don't know what it is about you," Clover breathed heavily, "but you bring out the lust in me."

"Lucky me," Fargo said, and inhaled her right nipple. She gasped and entwined her fingers in his hair while he sucked and tweaked and licked until both her breasts were heaving with excitement and desire.

They had the rest of the day to themselves so there was no need to rush. After nuzzling between her globes, Fargo ran the tip of his tongue from her cleavage to her navel. Again she shivered, and uttered a tiny laugh.

Planting light kisses on her belly, Fargo unfastened her britches and slid them down her satiny legs. They caught around her ankles and he had to tug to get them off.

"Careful there, muscles," Clover teased. "These happen to be the only pair of pants I own."

Fargo placed his hands on her shoulders and pressed her flat on her back beside him. The wanton gleam in her eyes matched his inner craving. He removed the rest of her clothes and sat back to admire her ravishing figure.

Country girls were generally more active than their city counterparts, their bodies more lithe and fit. Clover was no exception. Sinewy but undeniably enticing, she was the sort of woman lonely men dreamed about when they had no woman of their own. She was also as impatient as most of her gender.

"Are you going to sit there all day? I'd be awful disappointed."

Grinning, Fargo kissed her full on her hot lips. This time she sucked on his tongue, hers so exquisitely soft it was almost liquid. Ripples of pleasure coursed clear down to the tips of his toes.

"Mmmmmmm," Clover cooed when she drew back for breath. "You make my head swim."

Fargo kissed her cheek, her ear, her neck. He kissed the soft skin at the base of her throat, kissed her right breast and her left, and as he kissed he slid his right hand across the downy muff at the junction of her thighs, and then lower, to her waiting slit, so moist and warm.

"Oh, yes!" Clover exhaled. "I want you. I want you so much."

He parted her nether lips and stroked his forefinger across her swollen knob. It caused her to arch her body off the grass, her spine bent like a bow, her lips parted in a silent gasp. Her bottom moved, grinding into his palm with increasing vigor, while her thighs parted wider to grant him freer reign.

Fargo slowly slid a finger inside her and her inner walls rippled and wreathed him like a sheath. When he pumped his hand a few times, Clover suddenly clung to him and clasped her thighs tight while thrusting her bottom against him again and again and again. He felt her spurt, felt her whole body quake, felt her teeth sink into his shoulder.

"Ahhhhhhhhhhhhhh!"

Her cry wafted on the breeze. Out of habit Fargo looked up. The woods were as they should be: undisturbed and serene. The horses were grazing. He bent his mouth to her left breast and lightly nipped at her nipple.

His member was iron hard. As much as Fargo yearned to plunge it into her, he exercised sufficient self-control to wait, to hold off until the moment was right, until she wanted it so badly she was beside herself.

That moment was a long time coming. Clover matched the slow, sensuous rhythm of his thrusts, a wry smile curling her luscious lips. She contained her ardor so that they took forever coasting to the summit of pure and total passion. Her skin became as hot as fireplace coals, her moans rose nonstop to the leafy green boughs above, her nails raked his back and shoulders, occasionally drawing blood.

Fargo savored every second, much as a lover of fine

wine would savor every drop of a vintage year. He kissed every square inch of her face, neck and shoulders, and she repaid the favor many times over. He lathered her breasts until they were slick. She turned his ears into molten flames.

Their eventual release was all the more intense for the time it took them to reach it. Clover gushed first, her widening eyes betraying her. Her inner dam burst and she dug her nails into his biceps and voiced low, inarticulate mews and groans. Her thighs clamped harder, her ankles locked at the small of his back, and she came up off the grass in a frenzied orgasm. "Oh! Oh! Oh!" she said over and over as she spurted and spurted, drenching him with her excess.

For Fargo it was an earthquake and a volcanic eruption combined in one shattering climax. As always, the world around them blurred. As always, he was enveloped in a cloud of bliss. There was, in his opinion, no experience like it, and he would never get enough if he lived to be a hundred.

But all good things do indeed come to an end, and eventually Fargo stopped rocking and settled contentedly onto Clover's quivering melons. She bestowed tiny kisses in gratitude, and sank back. A languid smile showed that she had enjoyed herself as much as he had.

"You're the best."

Fargo wondered how many lovers she'd had but he did not bring it up. Women could be sensitive about things like that and he did not want to spoil the moment. Rolling onto his side, he draped an arm across her chest and closed his eyes. He could do with a nap and assumed she could, too. But just as he was on the cusp of dozing off, the Ovaro whinnied.

Own a horse long enough, ride it day after day, year after year, and a man grows to know the horse as well as he knows himself. He knows its habits, knows how it will act in practically any given situation. Knows the sounds it makes, and why. In this case, the Ovaro's whinny was one of alarm; someone or something was out there in the night, and the pinto was warning him.

Sitting up, Fargo gazed in the direction the stallion was gazing with its ears pricked and its nostrils flaring. He saw nothing, but the pinto's senses were far sharper than his. He ignored them at his peril. Swiftly dressing, he buckled on his gun belt and confirmed the Colt had five pills in the wheel. Like most frontiersmen, he kept the chamber under the hammer empty to avoid accidents.

Clover's eyes were shut but she sluggishly stirred when he stood up and his spurs jingled. "What is it, lover?"

"I don't know yet. Get dressed." Fargo slid the Henry from the saddle scabbard and worked the lever.

"Dressed?" Clover grumbled, and slowly rose onto an elbow. "Are we going somewhere?"

"We might have company."

That woke her up. Clover began pulling on clothes as fast as her fingers could fly. "Where?" she whispered. "Is it Bramwell and the men?"

"I don't know yet. Get under cover." Fargo moved toward the boulder-strewn hill, his gaze flitting from boulder to boulder, but whatever or whoever was up there was not in sight. Crouching behind the lowest, he waited for the person or beast to show themselves.

Clover, meanwhile, hurried toward the trees, dressing as she went, her breasts flouncing like gourds on a vine during a high wind.

Lingering tendrils of fatigue muddled Fargo's mind and he shook his head to dispel them. A hint of movement snapped him around to the left. Not forty feet distant a shadowy shape was slinking toward the bottom of the hill. A shape wearing a broad-brimmed black hat and a long black slicker.

The killer had found them.

It sparked a host of questions which Fargo would

deal with later. Right now he rested the Henry on the top of the boulder to steady his aim. Here was his chance to put an end to the bloodletting. Centering the front sight on the killer's silhouette, he aligned the rear sight and touched his finger to the trigger but he did not shoot. Not quite yet. Another couple of yards and the murderer would be in the open.

Inexplicably, the shadow halted. The black hat turned, and in the blink of an eye, the killer was gone, vanishing as if into thin air.

Fargo rose a little higher. Instantly there came a sharp *crack* and a slug ricocheted off the boulder. Stinging chips struck his cheek and forehead and he instinctively ducked down to spare his eyes.

Another rifle boomed. Clover had taken a shot at the killer, who retaliated by banging three rapid shots at her. Puffs of gun smoke pinpointed the boulder the killer was behind, and Fargo circled to the right to come up on it from the rear. He glanced toward Clover to see if she was all right and saw her flat on her belly, crawling from one tree to another. He hoped she had the common sense to stay low.

That the killer had found them told Fargo several things. First, whoever it was had tracked them there; he was positive they had not been followed. And since tracking wasn't a skill Philadelphia schoolteachers were noted for, there went his notion it might be Argent Meriwether.

Secondly, since it had taken the killer a good long while to overtake them, it meant the killer had started tracking well after their flight from Jacksonville. So either the killer had not been aware they had escaped until well after the fact, or else the killer had stumbled on their trail, recognized the Ovaro's tracks, and come after them.

And lastly, the fact that the killer was once again trying to slay them made Fargo think that the killer saw one or both of them as threats who must be disposed of as soon as possible. But Fargo was at a loss to explain why they were more of a threat than the rest of the Jackson clan.

The answer had to wait. Fargo was close to the boulder. He did not spot the killer, but high weeds next to it suggested where the rider in black had taken cover. Fargo half wished Clover would squeeze off a few more shots so the killer would return her fire and give himself away.

Suddenly, from higher up the hill, came the dull thud of a heavy hoof. Whirling, Fargo saw the big bay standing in the shadow of a gigantic slab of rock. Veering wide so the killer would not spot him, he climbed toward it.

Sooner or later the killer would return to his horse. All Fargo had to do was pick his spot, wait for the man in black to show, and that would be that. But the spot must be perfect.

Staying low, Fargo climbed well past the bay, hopped into a shallow gully, and crabbed sideways until he was directly above the horse. The woods were deceptively quiet, as if the wildlife was holding its collective breath. So was Fargo, but he didn't realize it until his lungs demanded air.

He did not take his eyes off the horse, which was staring at a stand of saplings fifteen yards from where the killer had last been. Why, was not hard to guess.

A moving shadow materialized and acquired form and substance. The Ozark terror was stealthily making for his mount, his black-clad body blending into the shadowed undergrowth.

Right away Fargo noticed something strange. The last time he saw the rider in black, he had been convinced it was a woman. But now he was not so sure. Men and women had different ways of moving and walking and running, and the killer was definitely moving as a man would.

Fargo did not have a clear shot. He impatiently

waited for the killer to raise his head a little higher so he could see who it was. A few more feet, and the man in black did just that. Disappointment knifed through him. A black bandanna covered most of the killer's face, the low brim of his hat the rest. All Fargo could see were the man's eyes, fixed on the bay. So be it. He would shoot him dead and find out who it was later. Fargo lowered a knee to the side of the gully to steady his aim, and without warning several pebbles clattered to the bottom.

The bay heard. It turned and whinnied, which was all it took to send the killer scurrying into the vegetation.

Fargo fired anyway. But just as his finger tightened on the trigger, the figure in black dived to the right and the slug meant to end his murderous spree struck a sapling, leaving a hole the size of a two-bit piece. Ejecting the spent cartridge, Fargo scoured the slope; when it came to woodcraft, the man was as adept as a Cherokee.

Fargo had to move. The killer knew where he was and would be working up the slope toward him. Crouching below the gully's rim, he followed it to where it slashed down the north face of the hill.

Living in the wild honed a man's patience. Stalking game required long hours of sitting and waiting. So did stalking men.

The bay whinnied again but Fargo did not turn his head. The slightest movement might give him away. Only his eyes moved, roving from one likely spot to the next. Sweat formed on his brow and trickled down his face but he ignored it.

Then saddle leather creaked and the bay nickered, and Fargo rose onto his knees to find the man in black reining the horse past a rock outcropping. He snapped off a shot but he knew even as he fired that he had missed, and he swore as hoofbeats rapidly dwindled into the distance.

"Skye!" Clover shouted. "He's gettin' away!"

No fooling, Fargo thought, and ran to the bottom of the hill, and their blankets. Swiftly he gathered up his saddle and saddle blanket and threw them on the Ovaro.

"We're going after him?" Clover excitedly asked.

"Not we. Me." Fargo had intended to sleep through the night and ride out at first light but there would be no rest for him. "I want you to go to Patrice's farm." It was the only place she would be safe.

Clover angrily tapped her foot. "Why can't I go with you? I promise I won't get in your way."

"No." Fargo said. He was only thinking of her. When he caught up with the killer, lead would fly fast and furious.

13

The tracks led in the direction of Jacksonville. For half an hour Fargo trotted hard, eager to catch up and do to the killer as the killer had tried twice now to do to him. He wanted to take Clover to the farm first but the time squandered would cost him the chance to end the bloodletting.

Fargo did not slow down or stop to rest until, of a sudden, he came to where the man in black had changed direction. Puzzled, Fargo drew rein. The killer was now traveling due west. But nothing lay in that direction except mile after mile of uninhabited wilderness.

A flick of his arm and Fargo was on the move again. Judging by the bay's gait, the man in black was in a hurry to get wherever he was going. Once, though, atop a wooded ridge, the killer had stopped. To check his back trail, Fargo suspected. He doubted the killer had spotted him, though, as thick as the vegetation was.

Another quarter of an hour went by. Then, once again, the bay changed direction, this time to the north. Fargo came to a halt and scratched his chin. There was nothing that way, either. He rode on and presently came to where the man in black had reined to the northeast. It was almost as if the killer were riding in a giant circle.

That was when it hit him, when Fargo stiffened as if jolted by a bolt of lightning and cursed himself for being the biggest jackass this side of creation. The killer *was* riding in a circle, back to the spring and the boulder-strewn hill.

It couldn't be coincidence. As Fargo was learning to his dismay, everything the man in black did, he did for a reason. And there was only one reason the killer would be heading back to the spring. He was after Clover.

The man in black had counted on Fargo coming after him. Had counted, too, on Fargo coming after him alone to make better time. The killer knew Clover was now alone and unprotected.

Fargo could only hope she had done as he had told her and by now was halfway to Patrice's place. If not, well, Fargo did not finish the thought. But he did silently vow that if anything happened to her, he would not rest until he personally bucked the killer out in gore.

The suspense gnawed at Fargo's insides like termites gnawing at wood. It was almost as bad as the shame of being outwitted yet again. Fargo had never claimed to be the smartest hombre alive, but usually his wits were sharp enough for him to hold his own against most anyone. The man in black, however, was outguessing him at every turn. It was downright humiliating and Fargo did not like being humiliated. He did not like it one damn bit.

Presently, Fargo came to where the killer had slowed to approach the glade. He did not slow. Rising in the stirrups, he spied the spring but did not see any sign of the man in black or of Clover. A last spurt of speed carried him out of the trees.

His fear had been well founded. Clover's saddle was where it had been when he left. The upended coffee pot lay in the grass. So did the tin cup Clover had used, lying next to the burlap bag.

There was evidence of a struggle. Vaulting down, Fargo studied the sign, reconstructing the events in his mind's eye.

Clover had taken her sweet time getting ready to leave. She had decided to have a cup of coffee before riding out, and had added a few limbs to the fire. Then she had sat with her back to the woods, waiting for the coffeepot to heat up. She probably never heard the killer dismount at the glade's edge. The first inkling she had that she was in danger came when the killer seized her from behind. She had put up a fight but the killer prevailed, carried her to the mare, and threw her across it without bothering to saddle up.

Had she been alive or dead at that point? The way Fargo saw it, the man in black wouldn't bother to cart off a body unless it was to secretly dispose of it, so there was a good chance Clover had been alive. But for how long?

The killer was leading the mare by the reins and could not travel fast. They were only ten minutes ahead, if that. Fargo swiftly mounted, and riding like a reckless bat out of hell, he covered half a mile at breakneck speed.

The tracks skirted a knoll. Rounding it, Fargo noticed a particularly large tree to his left. He was almost even with it, his eyes glued to the ground and the tracks, when he sensed movement and snapped his head around. The horror he beheld caused him to yank on the reins harder than he ever had.

Clover was dangling from the end of a rope tied to a limb. Her face was beet red and she was frantically but weakly tearing at the noose, her legs twitching and trembling in the last throes before death.

"No!" Fargo cried. Sharply reining the Ovaro, he came over next to her, unhooked his boots from the stirrups, placed them flat on his saddle, and stood up, drawing the Arkansas Toothpick from its ankle sheath as he rose. The Ovaro, thankfully, stood perfectly still.

One slash was all it took. The rope parted and Fargo wrapped both arms around Clover to keep her from falling. Her extra weight, though, caused the pinto to shift, and he was unable to keep his balance. As they fell, he twisted so that he bore the brunt of impact with his left shoulder. Pain spiked through him but he disregarded it and rolled Clover onto her back.

The noose had bitten into her flesh. Her face was purple and her eyes were rolling up in her head and her limbs had gone completely limp.

Desperately, Fargo pried at the noose and succeeded in loosening it enough to cut it with the Toothpick. But she had stopped breathing. Placing one hand on top of the other on her chest as he had seen someone do with a drowning victim, he pushed as hard as he could and then let up, declaring, "Live, damn it!" She did not respond. He did it again, and when there still was no reaction, he shifted his hands to her stomach and bore down with his full weight.

A gasp escaped Clover's lips. Her eyes opened and she shrieked in terror, struggling for breath.

"It's me," Fargo said. "You're safe now."

Sucking in loud, ragged breaths, Clover quivered and groaned. Gradually her face lost its purple cast. Breathing normally, she tried to sit up but collapsed. Her hands fluttered to her throat. She tried to speak but all that came out were guttural noises more befitting a stricken animal.

"Lie still," Fargo coaxed. "Give yourself time."

Clover nodded and licked her dry lips. She began coughing and nearly doubled over, then straightened and weakly smiled to show she was all right.

Fargo glanced up. He yearned to go after the man in black but that was out of the question now. He must tend to Clover before anything else. The hour of reckoning had to wait.

Crackling in the underbrush brought Fargo around in a blur. He drew as he turned, hoping the killer had returned. But it was only the mare. Holstering the Colt, he sank back down.

"Thank you," Clover croaked.

"You shouldn't talk yet," Fargo said. "Your throat must be sore as hell."

"It is. But if not for you, I would be a lot worse off." Clover gingerly ran her fingers along the raw gash. "I can't believe he did it."

"Did you recognize him?"

"No," Clover said. "His face was covered except for his eyes and when he spoke he disguised how he really sounds by talkin' in a deep, low voice." She winced and lowered her arm. "There was something about him, though, something I can't quite put my finger on."

"Maybe it will come to you," Fargo said hopefully.

"Maybe." Clover coughed some more. "You should have heard him. He laughed as he strung me up. He didn't tie my hands because he wanted me to struggle. He wanted me to scream and kick."

"It's best you don't talk about it."

"No, I'd rather I did," Clover disagreed. "He had a pistol to my head the whole time he was tightening the noose. Then he slapped the mare, and when she ran out from under me, he pulled on the rope to haul me higher." She shuddered at the memory and started to turn her head to look at the tree but, instead clenched her teeth and groaned. "It hurts something awful."

"I keep saying you should lie still," Fargo said. Not that she would listen; since when did women ever take a man's advice?

"You should have heard him braggin'," Clover said. "About how many of us he's killed. About how before he's through, there won't be a Jackson left alive." She swallowed a few times. "And right before he slapped the mare, he made a strange comment."

"Which was?"

"He said, 'One more for love'." Clover slowly sat up. "What do you suppose he meant?"

Fargo shrugged. He had no idea.

"Is murderin' us some kind of game with him?" Clover wondered. "Is he a lunatic or is there more to this than we've imagined?"

Again Fargo shrugged. The more he learned, the more the mystery deepened. But one thing he did know. As soon as he had her safely tucked away he would find the answers he needed or there would be hell to pay. "Let's get you to the spring. I'll tend your neck, and as soon as you're fit for a long ride, we'll head for the farm."

"You're not going after him?" Clover struggled up onto her elbows. "Don't stay on my account. Go, now, while he doesn't have much of a lead."

Fargo had made the mistake of leaving her alone once. He would not make it again. "You're more important."

Clover smiled through her pain. "Has anyone ever told you that you are a kitten at heart?"

"Not in this lifetime, no," Fargo said. He had been called a bastard once or twice, a son of a bitch now and then, but never a kitten. "Let me help you." He slid an arm under hers and boosted her to her feet. For a few seconds she swayed, clinging to his arm. Then she thrust out her chin, pushed his arm away, and stepped to the mare under her own power. He was ready to help her climb on but she managed it alone. "You're one tough lady."

"Got that right," Clover said, and smiled.

To avoid adding to her discomfort, Fargo held to a walk the whole way back. He spread out her blankets and bundled one of his for a pillow. Then, while she gratefully rested, he cut a strip from another blanket, soaked it in the spring, and gently applied it to her neck.

"That feels good."

Fargo filled the coffeepot and prepared a fresh batch of coffee. Aware of her eyes on him, he glanced up. "What?"

"I was just thinkin' that it's a shame you'll never set down roots."

Fargo let it pass without comment. From his saddlebags he took several pieces of pemmican. "Here. It's almost as good as mountain lion." Which he had eaten a few times and found it the tastiest meat ever.

"You would never catch me eatin' painter," Clover declared. "It would be as terrible as eatin' a dog."

Fargo didn't mention he had done that, too. Among some Indian tribes dog meat was highly prized. If a visitor refused to eat it, it was taken as an insult.

Clover nibbled a bit, then ran a hand across her eyes. "I feel awful tired. Would you mind if I slept a while?"

"Don't be silly." Fargo armed himself with the Henry. "While you're resting I'll rustle up something for supper."

"Just so it's not mountain lion." Clover was so worn out she was asleep seconds after she closed her eyes.

Fargo covered her to her chin with a blanket, set her rifle by her side in case she should need it, and went to the spring. He had his choice of a game trail regularly used by deer at dawn and dusk when they came to drink and a rabbit run that wound off among the boulders. He chose the rabbit run. Forty yards up he made himself comfortable on a flat-topped boulder and settled down to wait.

An hour passed. Two hours. A pair of jays came to the spring to drink and flew off squawking. A robin hunted for worms in the soft soil at the water's edge. A box turtle waddled out of the high grass, sat staring a while, and waddled back into the grass without slaking its thirst.

Finally a long-eared bolt of brown came bounding down the hill. A male rabbit in its prime, it stopped to test the wind. Its long ears swivelled from side to side and it raised its head, its nose twitching, seeking a telltale scent that would send it scurrying into hiding.

In order not to ruin any of the meat, Fargo shot it through the head, not the heart. Sliding off the boulder, Fargo picked it up by the back legs and carried it to the fire. He took a whetstone from his saddlebags and honed the Arkansas Toothpick to a razor's edge. The skinning was done in no time; he had skinned so many rabbits, he could do it in his sleep. When he was done, he cut the meat into chunks and impaled them on a thin branch that he rigged over the fire on a spit.

Rummaging in the burlap bag to see what else Clover had brought, Fargo found several potatoes. He placed them near the flames to bake, then sat back. Soon the aroma had his mouth watering and his stomach grumbling.

When he tried to wake Clover, all she did was mumble and smack her lips and go right on sleeping. He tried again, gently shaking her arm, but she did not stir. Figuring it was better for her to rest, he placed the rabbit and the potatoes on the burlap bag to cool.

Stifling a yawn, Fargo stood. He was tired but he had learned his lesson. The man in black was not to be taken lightly. He made a circuit of the clearing to satisfy himself the killer had not doubled back, then selected a shaded tree that offered an unobstructed view of the clearing and the hill, and sat with his back to the trunk.

It was nine o'clock that night before Clover stirred. She groaned a few times, then slowly sat up, a hand to her forehead. "Skye?"

The flames had long since gone out and she did not see him until he was right next to her. "It's me," Fargo assured her when she recoiled in fright, and hunkered to rekindle the fire. "Are you hungry?"

"Am I ever. I could even eat a mountain lion." Her teeth flashed white in the darkness.

A while later, after they had gorged on rabbit and baked potatoes and Fargo was licking his fingers clean, Clover looked at him across the fire and asked, "What are your plans for tomorrow?"

"You don't want to know."

"Why not?"

His answer would only upset her so Fargo did not answer. Come the new day, and he would do unto others as they had been doing to him. The hill folk had only themselves to blame. They thought they could do as they pleased and get away with it.

They were in for one hellacious rude awakening.

14

The two women posted as sentries at the mouth of the valley were doing what all the other women had done: they were talking when they should have been keeping an eye out for unwanted visitors. The first inkling they had that Fargo was there came when he stepped from the undergrowth with the Colt in his hand. "Morning, ladies."

Prudence was one of them. She lunged for the rifle she had carelessly leaned against a tree but she froze when she heard him thumb back the Colt's hammer.

"I don't want to shoot you but I will if you force me," Fargo bluntly informed them. "It's your choice."

They chose wisely. Hands in the air, they nervously watched him throw one of their rifles into the brush. Prudence's rifle he held on to, cradling it under his arm. Neither woman wore a gun belt or had a knife.

"I can't believe you had the gall to show your face here again," Prudence angrily declared. "Argent warned you what would happen if you didn't stay away."

"I don't take to threats," Fargo said. Stepping back, he said over his shoulder, "You can come out now."

The undergrowth parted and Clover rode into the open, leading the Ovaro by the reins.

"Sister Clover!" Prudence exclaimed. "We feared you were dead!"

"I darn near was," Clover responded. "I've found out who has been doing all the killin' and it's not who we think." She nodded at Fargo. "This man is my friend. He's saved my hide several times over, and I don't want you givin' him trouble."

"But Argent said—" the other woman began. She was big-boned and had shoulders almost as wide as a man's.

Clover cut her off. "Does she do your thinkin' for you now, Bernice? I tell you this man is our friend, and I'll shoot anyone who tries to plant him." She leveled her rifle. "Try me and see if I don't."

Prudence was looking from Fargo to Clover and back again. "You're one of the best friends I've had, and if you vouch for this handsome drink of water, I'll take your word for it. But Argent won't be so easy to convince."

Fargo swung onto the stallion. "Leave Argent Meriwether to me."

"I don't like the sound of that," Bernice said.

"Think highly of her, do you?" Fargo asked, not really caring but wanting to take Bernice's measure.

"Damned right I do! She's helped open our eyes. Helped us see how downtrodden we were, without us even realizin' it. She's a suffragist, you know. She believes women should have the same rights men do, and by God, we will one day! It's only fair."

Fargo remembered hearing somewhere that women in some of the larger cities back East had banded together to demand they be given the right to vote. If Meriwether was indeed a suffragist, as they were known, it explained a lot. "And how fair is it to blame the men in your clan for something they didn't do?"

"You know this for a fact, do you?" Bernice snapped.

Clover spoke up. "*I* do. I've seen the killer with my own eyes. He strung me up and left me for dead."

She moved the strip of blanket covering the gash in her neck. "See for yourselves."

"Good God!" Prudence exclaimed. "You must have had a real good look at him. Who is it?"

"Most of his face was covered," Clover said.

Bernice's mouth quirked in a sneer. "Then for all you know, it *could* be someone from our clan."

"Or someone who isn't a Jackson," Fargo mentioned, but they ignored him.

"You weren't there," Clover addressed her cousins. "You haven't talked to Porter and Bramwell like I have. I'm tellin' you, the men have nothin' to do with any of this. We only think they do."

Bernice wasn't satisfied. "Give me one shred of evidence and I'll believe you. But as things stand, nothin' you've said has changed my mind."

Fargo nipped an argument in the bud by saying, "You can hash it out later. Right now you two ladies are going to do us a favor."

"Like Hades we are," Bernice said, then could not resist asking, "What kind of favor?"

"There's another sentry between here and the farmhouse," Fargo said. "You're going to help us get past her."

"Not in a million years," Bernice said, shaking her head. "I won't betray my sisters this side of dyin'."

Fargo was prepared for this. In order to end the bloodshed, drastic steps were called for. Such as the one he took next. Ordinarily, he would never strike a woman unless gravely provoked, but lives were at stake. So, without saying another word, he walked up to Bernice Jackson and punched her in the gut. Not all that hard, certainly nowhere near as hard as he would slug a man in a fistfight. Even so, the blow doubled her over.

Gurgling and groaning, Bernice tottered as spittle dribbled over her lower lip.

"I wasn't *asking* you," Fargo said. "I was *telling* you."

Prudence was as mad as a wet cat. Fidgeting anxiously, she growled, "Damn you, mister! You had no call to do that."

"I want your word that you'll do exactly as I tell you," Fargo said.

"Please," Clover interjected. "Do as he says. It's for the best for all of us."

"What if we're not as trustin' as you?" Prudence balked. "What if we refuse to go along?"

Fargo touched the Colt's muzzle to Bernice's temple. "Then I'll shoot her in the head." He was playing another bluff but they didn't know that. And the worried expression Clover cast at him showed that she wasn't so sure, either. "You have until I count to five to make up your mind." He paused. "One."

Bernice clutched at Prudence's leg. "Don't give in on my account! Think of Argent and the others."

"Two," Fargo said.

Prudence's face was a mask of indecision. "I don't want to betray Argent but I don't want the killin's to go on, either."

"Three."

Wiping a sleeve across her mouth, Bernice unfolded. "Don't you dare! I don't care what happens to me. He mustn't reach the farmhouse."

Fargo felt like he did when he raised a poker pot with nothing but a pair of twos in his hands. "That makes four," he counted, and spread his other hand close to the Colt to give the impression he did not want blood to splatter on him.

"All right!" Prudence blurted. "I give you my word. I'll do whatever you want. Just don't shoot her."

In frustration, Bernice hit her own thigh. "Dang it all. Didn't anything I say sink in? It's Argent who matters most."

"That's where you're wrong," Prudence said. "Our

clan comes before all else. Blood is thicker than high-falutin words. I'm willin' to play this out for the good of all the Jacksons."

"Well, I'm sure as hell not," Bernice said, and spinning with surprising speed, she raced down the trail.

Counting on Clover to keep an eye on Prudence, Fargo went after Bernice on foot. He expected to catch up within moments but she was a lot faster than she looked. He fairly flew but he could not gain ground, and if he didn't, if she reached the valley floor before he did and shouted a warning, it would dash any hope he had of reaching the farmhouse unchallenged.

Bernice glanced over her shoulder as she rounded the next bend. She wasn't watching where she was going and veered off the trail into the trees. She immediately veered back again but a bush blocked her path and when she tried to avoid it, her foot became entangled and she pitched on to her stomach. "No!" she cried out.

Fargo reached her as she was rising and grabbed her left arm. Wrenching free, she lurched away. He snagged her shirt, bringing her to a stop, but if he thought that was the end of it, he was mistaken.

Hissing like an alley cat, Bernice whirled and clawed at his face and eyes with her fingernails hooked like talons. She was beside herself with fury, and she lit into him like a wildcat gone berserk.

Taken off guard, Fargo was slashed across the cheek, then the neck. It stung like hell, and he felt the damp trickle of his own blood. "Calm down!" he hollered, but she was past the point of listening to reason. Again she slashed at him, at his eyes. He avoided losing his eyesight by the width of a cat's whisker.

"I'll kill you!" Bernice shrieked, and buried her fingernails in his neck. Her shoulder muscle bunching, she tried to rip his throat out.

That was the last straw. Fargo brought the Colt crashing down on her head. But once again he did not use his full strength, and instead of collapsing, Bernice staggered, growled, and came at him again. Fargo raised a forearm to ward her off but she grabbed hold and clung to him with surprising tenacity, seeking to trip him and pull him down with her. He tried to shake her off and when that failed, he hooked his boot behind her legs and pushed, tripping her. He thought she would let go to cushion her fall but instead she held on and flung a leg around his ankles.

Fargo stayed on his feet, but now he was bent over and off balance, and worse, his face and throat were inches from her face and her teeth.

Opening her mouth wide, Bernice attempted to sink her teeth into his jugular. Fargo jerked back and she missed. He pushed against her but he could not break her hold. The next second she bit down with all her might on his wrist, and excruciating pain shot through him.

Fargo punched her but the blow had no effect. Her fingernails were gouging deeper into his neck; at any moment she might sever a vein. Left with no choice, he drew back the Colt to pistol-whip her. She would be bruised for days, maybe weeks, but she would live, and that was the important thing.

But as his arm swept down, Bernice's other leg swept out, catching him in a scissors hold. By sheer brute strength Fargo pulled his left leg free but he could not extricate his right. When Bernice suddenly twisted her whole body, his leg was pulled out from under him, and down he went. She did not give him a second's respite. Partly rising, she hurled herself at him with renewed ferocity.

Fargo had been in some tough fights. He had slugged it out with mountains of muscle twice his size and with men who rained punches faster than a striking rattler. But few matched Bernice Jackson for sheer savagery. Again her raking nails seared his flesh, and at that, Fargo lost control. He pushed up off the grass and she clung to him like before, her teeth rising toward his neck. Once, twice, three times he slugged her on the jaw, and at the third *crunch,* she sprawled flat, blood trickling from the corners of her mouth.

Fargo stepped back. His face and neck were a welter of cuts and scrapes. He had forgotten about the Colt and jammed it into his holster. Taking deep breaths to still the raging in his veins, he squatted, lifted her, and slung her over his right shoulder. He didn't care that her cheek struck his shoulder blade or that her shirt had come half undone.

Clover took one look and blurted, "Land sakes! You look like someone carved on you with a sword."

Prudence was more concerned for Bernice. "What did you do to her? Is she alive?" She took a step but something in Fargo's expression stopped her from coming any closer.

Lowering Bernice to the ground, Fargo walked to the Ovaro, took his rope from his saddle, and wrapped Bernice in a rope cocoon. He added a gag, then dragged her into a batch of weeds. "Now where were we?" Picking up Prudence's rifle, he emptied it and shoved it at Prudence.

"What am I supposed to do with this?"

"Point it at us." Blinking blood from his eye, Fargo climbed onto the Ovaro. His eyebrow was bleeding, one of a dozen deep cuts. When he pressed his sleeve to it, the buckskin came away bright red.

"I get it," Prudence said. "You want to pretend I've taken you prisoner so no one will stop us."

"That's the general idea." Fargo drew his Colt and pointed it at her. "You're a smart lady. So I don't need to tell you what will happen if you try to warn them."

"They would blast you from your horse," Prudence predicted with relish.

"But I'll take three or four of them with me before I go down," Fargo vowed. "Is that what you want?"

Prudence bit her lower lip.

In single file they entered the valley, Clover in front on the mare, Prudence walking to one side of the Ovaro with the empty rifle trained on them, Fargo with one hand up under his shirt, training the Colt on her.

"You're doing the right thing," Clover said.

"To tell you the truth, I don't know what is right anymore," Prudence said. "I just want to be with my husband again."

As they neared the stand of trees at the valley's midpoint, the sandy-haired sentry stood up and waved.

"Wave back," Fargo told Prudence, "and smile."

The sentry let them go on by.

"It worked!" Clover whispered, and giggled.

But she was being premature. Fargo had seen the sentry coming toward them, the squirrel rifle in the crook of her elbow.

"Hold up there, Sister Prudence!" the sandy-haired woman hollered. "Where's Sister Bernice?"

Prudence was equal to the occasion. "Guarding the trail, Sister Lilith. We figured one of us should stay. It wouldn't do to leave it unprotected."

"Do you need help escortin' them in?"

"No. I can manage. But I thank you."

That satisfied Lilith, who nodded and smiled and went back into the trees.

Ahead was the farmhouse. Women were moving about. A number of children were playing tag.

On his last visit Fargo had bent over backward to show Argent Meriwether and her followers that he meant them no harm. In return, they had taken his guns and run him off. This time would be different.

Fargo was through being nice.

15

As they approached the farmhouse Fargo wedged the Colt under his belt and slid his right hand from under his shirt. Once again the women and children converged to meet them, and once again Argent Meriwether came barreling out of the house like a bull from a holding pen.

"Clover! You're back safe and sound! We were worried." Argent beamed and spread her arms wide.

Clover dismounted, her rifle in hand, and stood still as the other woman enfolded her in a bear hug. "Have you heard about Harriet?"

None of the women, Fargo was glad to note, were pointing weapons at him. They mistakenly believed Prudence had him covered. He slowly dismounted and slid his hand back up under his shirt to the Colt.

"We found her body," Argent said saying. "The men will pay for these atrocities, I promise you." She glanced at Prudence. "That will be all. You can head back to your post."

Prudence hesitated.

Since Fargo could not trust her to keep quiet, he had to act. Whirling, he sprang behind Meriwether and clamped one arm around her throat while jamming the Colt against her temple. Momentarily too shocked to resist, she recovered her wits and grabbed at his arm but by then he had her at his mercy. "Don't even think it," he warned.

Some of the women started forward but stopped. Several raised rifles but did not dare shoot.

"Ladies," Fargo said amiably, "we've been through this once before so you know how it goes. Drop your weapons or I splatter her brains." He wouldn't shoot her but they didn't know that.

No one complied. They looked at one another, each waiting for the other to do something. Most were non-plussed when Clover suddenly stepped to Fargo's side and pointed her rifle at them.

"You heard him, sisters! Do as he says and we'll live through the day."

Evangeline found her voice. "What in the world is going on here, Clover? You're sidin' with him against us?"

"There's more to it," Clover said. "All we want is to talk to Argent in private. I give you my word as your kinsman she won't be harmed."

Argent started to struggle but desisted when Fargo gouged the barrel into her skin. "Don't listen to her, sisters! Don't listen to either of them! Shoot them down like the dogs they are."

Whispers spread, and Evangeline stepped forward. "No, Sister Argent, we won't risk losing you. So long as they don't lift a finger against you, we won't lift ours against them."

"I thought I taught you better!" Argent spat in disgust. "We must never show weakness to this man or any other!"

Fargo began backing toward the farmhouse. It would not be wise to let her incite them. "That's enough out of you."

Evidently Clover had the same thought. "Everyone keep their heads," she advised. "All of you know me. All of you know I only have our best interests at heart. So stay calm."

Fargo thought some of them would resort to their

guns anyway but he made it to the porch without a shot being fired. Reaching behind him, he opened the screen door. The inner door was already open. Several quick steps and he was inside, pushing Meriwether toward a settee. "Have a seat."

Clover closed both doors. "I'll check the house to be sure we're alone."

"Traitor," Argent hissed. "I'll see that you are cast from the sisterhood for your treachery."

"Sisterhood?" Fargo repeated.

"Any woman who joins the fight for suffrage is my sister in arms," Argent said. "We are soldiers for right, and we will not be denied."

"Is that what your war with the men is about?"

"Of course not," Argent said scornfully. "Much more is involved, as you must know by now." She tilted her chin in proud defiance. "But if, along the way, I can enlighten these ignorant crackers, so much the better."

"I've heard you were a suffragist," Fargo mentioned.

"One of the foremost in Philadelphia," Argent asserted. "My speeches always drew over a hundred women. Another ten years, and I'd have ten times that number turning out."

"Yet you gave all that up to come here. To live among a bunch of ignorant crackers, as you just called them."

"They are backward. They are uneducated and uncouth. There is no denying that. Had I not come, these women would still be wallowing in ignorance and sloth. I have done them a great service. I am educating them, broadening their horizons, bringing them out of the Dark Ages into the light of a new and modern era."

Fargo had met a lot of people who were naturally full of themselves but Argent Meriwether was in a class by herself.

"It would not be remiss to regard me as their savior," Argent went on. "As a beacon of hope and truth, to them and to the world."

"You put your pants on one leg at a time, the same as everyone else," Fargo remarked.

Argent stabbed a finger at him. "I wouldn't expect a bumpkin like you to grasp the importance of my life's mission. But I know whereof I speak. I was born into poverty, just like these women. I was forced to endure a childhood of shame and want, just like these women. I had men lording it over me from dawn until dusk, just like these women. But no more."

"The men aren't as bad as you make them out to be," Fargo said as he stepped to a window and peered out. The women were huddled in a large group, talking and gesturing.

"The men are worse!" Argent huffed. "Women must always bow and scrape to them, must always do what they want. We are not permitted to think for ourselves."

In addition to the settee there was a table with four chairs, a cabinet, and a clock on the wall. It was half-past ten. "A lot of men treat women with kindness," Fargo said.

"Oh, sure, the kindness of a lord to his slave. But that's neither here nor there. What matters is that the men of this clan murdered Elly for defying their wishes, and we took up arms in our own self-defense."

At that moment Clover came down the hall. "I'm not so sure about that anymore, Sister Argent. It could be that someone is playin' both sides for fools." She glanced at Fargo. "There's no one here but us. The back door is bolted and all the windows are shut."

"Good." Outside, two women were running toward the barn. Fargo wondered what that was about, and was glad to see the Ovaro had drifted to a patch of grass northwest of the house and was grazing.

Argent slid to the edge of the settee. "What are you talking about, Sister Clover? We all know Porter had Elly and Billy killed, and he's been killing ever since."

"Has he been killin' the men too? Because a lot of them have been murdered," Clover revealed. "I was there when Harriet was shot. We were bushwhacked by someone who also shot Bramwell and killed Jesse. Would Porter shoot his own son and his own nephew? I think not."

"Maybe it was an accident," Argent said. "In the dark people make mistakes."

"There was a fire burnin'," Clover set her straight. "And I saw the man who did it. He rides a big bay and goes around dressed all in black."

"You saw the killer with your own eyes? There can be no mistake?"

"None whatsoever," Clover assured her. "Skye saw him, too. They traded shots but the polecat got away."

"Twice," Fargo said in disgust.

"Well, this certainly puts everything in a whole new light," Argent said. "I'll have to give it serious thought."

"What is there to think about?" Clover asked. "Send someone to Porter under a white flag. Arrange a meetin' and share what we've learned. It could end the killin' and return things to how they were."

"Do you think Porter will listen?" Argent asked. "He's made no secret that he hates my guts and wants every rebel dead."

The two women who ran off had reappeared leading a saddled horse. One climbed on and galloped hell-bent for leather toward the trail out of the valley. Fargo felt it did not bode well.

"Maybe Porter will, maybe he won't," Clover said, "but we have to try. Lives are at stake."

"I don't know," Argent said. "Porter doesn't strike me as being in his right mind. It seems to me the best thing for us to do is stay the course until either he comes to his senses or this mysterious man in black is caught."

Clover moved closer. "And how many more people will die before then? Five? Ten? Twenty? We must do *something* and we must do it now."

"You're being hasty. You're thinking with your heart instead of your head. For all we know, this man in black is doing Porter's bidding."

"That's ridiculous."

"Is it?" Argent rested her hands on her knees. "Our minds work in devious ways, and no one is more devious than the head of your clan. Didn't you tell me that back in North Carolina he outwitted the leader of the Harker clan and nearly wiped the Harkers out?"

"Well, yes, but—"

"No buts about it," Argent said. "Porter has proven many times over that he has a murderous disposition. It's no great stretch to imagine he is the mastermind behind these latest atrocities."

Fargo hated to say it but Meriwether had a point. It could well be that Porter was somehow involved.

"So I don't see where taking me prisoner has changed anything," Argent stated. "I should resent it but I'm prepared to be lenient. You always have been one of my favorites." She reached out and placed a hand on Clover's. "One of my very special favorites."

"I'm plumb flattered," Clover said, "but it doesn't change things for me, either. I still aim to end the bloodshed no matter what it takes, with or without your help."

Frosty resentment twisted Argent's face. "What are you saying? That you won't do as I ask?"

"If you won't listen then I'll go have a talk with Porter," Clover proposed. "He shut his ears last time but maybe I can make him open them."

"You are deluding yourself, my dear."

"If it was your clan, you would understand," Clover said.

Argent's eyes glittered like those of a wolverine about to pounce. "I resent the insinuation. Would I have endured all I have on behalf of you and the other women if I did not have your clan's welfare at heart?"

Things were happening outside. The children were being whisked away. A redhead Fargo had not seen before was issuing instructions to women who were fanning out around the farmhouse. "Who's that?" he asked.

Clover came to the window. "Patrice. Elly was her daughter, remember? This is her farm and she knows it inside out."

Which told Fargo she might know a way in they had not thought of. "Is there a root cellar? Or a basement?"

"I know what you're thinkin', and no. To get in they'll have to break down a door or bust out a window."

The soft scrape of a shoe caused Fargo to whirl. Argent was almost to the hallway. She instantly bolted toward the rear of the house.

"After her!" Clover cried.

Not that Fargo needed any prompting. They were safe only so long as they had Argent. Should she escape, the other women would be on them like a swarm of riled hornets. For a teacher she was remarkably swift. She reached the kitchen, and the back door, well ahead of him. She threw the bolt and had her hand on the latch when Fargo gripped her by the shoulder and spun her around. "You're not going anywhere."

If Fargo expected her to meekly submit, he had another think coming. Venting a howl of fury, Meriwether hurled herself at him with the savagery of a riled grizzly. But where Bernice had used her fingernails to good effect, Argent relied on her fists. The notion might seem comical to some but her first blow disabused Fargo of the idea she would be easy to take down. It staggered him.

Argent grabbed the Henry and tried to rip it from his hands but couldn't.

"That's enough!" Clover yelled, aiming her rifle.

"You won't shoot me!" the teacher replied, and whipped her right fist in a backhand that caught Fargo in the cheek. Again she attempted to tear the Henry from his grasp. "Give it to me, damn you!"

"Like hell," Fargo said, and belted her. He held back but the blow still lifted her onto her heels. She made another feeble try to take the Henry, then her legs melted from under her and she wound up in an ungainly heap.

"We should tie her," Clover said.

Fargo was bending to drag Meriwether back to the sitting room when the crash of glass at the front of the house sent him running down the hall. A rock had been hurled through a window. Wary not to show himself, he peered out.

Patrice Jackson and Prudence and five others were only a few yards from the porch. "What in God's name is going on in there?" Patrice demanded. "We heard yellin'!"

"Everything is fine," Clover responded.

"Prove it!" Patrice challenged her. "Bring Argent to the window or the door so we can see with our own eyes she's all right."

Clover dropped her voice to a whisper. "What do we do? If we don't produce her, they might storm the house."

"We'll trick them," Fargo said, and hastened to the kitchen. Kneeling, he eased Argent over his shoulder and hurriedly retraced his steps. Holding her about the waist so her back was against his chest, he nodded at Clover and moved near enough to the window for the women outside to see her. But only for a few seconds. He did not want them to get too good a look.

"Satisfied?" Clover yelled.

"I don't know what you're tryin' to pull," was Patrice's reply, "but you're about to regret it."

16

Fargo did not expect the women to open fire. Not so long as Argent Meriwether was inside. But the next moment Patrice threw back her head and yelled, "Now, sisters, now!" and from all four sides of the house came a ragged volley. A withering storm of lead pelted the walls and windows.

Pulling the schoolmarm down beside him, Fargo flattened as glass shards rained down. The other window in the room shattered, pelting Clover. Slugs struck the inner walls and a few struck the ceiling and floor with the staccato cadence of hail.

Clover was on her hands and knees, her forearms over her head to ward off a shower of slivers and chips. "Stop firing! Please!" she shouted, but either no one heard, or no one cared.

The shooting stopped. In the heavy silence that followed, Fargo heard Patrice command the women to reload. Dragging Meriwether to the middle of the room, he left her and crawled back to the window.

As brazen as life, Patrice was right out in the open. "Are you still alive in there, outsider?"

"No thanks to you," Fargo replied. "You almost killed Clover and the teacher. Or doesn't that matter?"

"Clover is a traitor to her gender and deserves whatever she gets," Patrice said. "As for Sister Argent, she has often mentioned how she would gladly give her life to see justice done."

"You call this justice?" Fargo demanded. "Gunning people down in cold blood?" So long as he kept her talking, the women wouldn't resume firing.

"We're only doing as has been done to us," Patrice justified her side of the dispute. "Porter started this when he killed my Elly. The sweetest bundle of life you ever saw, stabbed to death in her prime."

"I had nothing to do with your daughter's death," Fargo said, but she did not seem to hear.

"My only child. My wonderful pride and joy," Patrice said softly, overcome by sorrow. "Every time I think of it, I get so twisted inside, I can't hardly think."

"Were you the one who found the bodies?"

Patrice nodded. "Billy was at the front of the barn, she was at the back. I think she tried to hide in some bales of hay. Both of them, so cut and hacked, you couldn't recognize their faces. Billy was the worse. His nose and ears were cut off, and the killer did unspeakable things to his body."

Fargo did not think highly of Porter Jackson but he did not see him as a butcher. He commented to that effect to Patrice.

"You're forgettin' something, mister," she said. "His knife was found near their bodies, caked with their blood."

"How can you be sure the knife was Porter's?"

"Because it was one he carried since he was a boy. His pa made it for him. It had a bone handle with Porter's initials carved into it. No one else owns one anything like it."

Which left two possibilities, to Fargo's way of thinking. One was that Porter really did the killings. The other he phrased in a question. "Couldn't someone have stolen his knife to place the blame on him?"

Patrice gestured. "That's what he claimed. But I didn't believe it then and I don't believe it now."

"Why not?"

She took another couple of steps, spitting her next words. "Because Porter never let that knife out of his sight. He always wore it in a sheath right here." She smacked the front of her right thigh. "His wife constantly complained that he even slept with the damn thing, and went on and on about how it would poke her all the time."

"But what if someone did steal it?" Fargo persisted.

Patrice regained some of her composure. "I expect this from you, seein' as how you're male and males always stick together even when they're in the wrong."

"Is that you talking or Argent Meriwether?" Fargo asked, merely to make a point, but he also made a mistake.

At the mention of the teacher, Patrice tried to peer past him into the room. "Where is she, anyhow? Why hasn't she said anything? So help me, if you've harmed a hair on her head, I will personally cut off your oysters and feed them to you a piece at a time."

"She's alive and well," Fargo said. He did not add that she was unconscious and bleeding.

"I'll make a deal with you, outsider. Send her out, and we'll let Clover and you ride away. What do you say?"

A brunette over behind a buckboard poked her head out. "Patrice! You can't! Argent wouldn't want you to and neither do most of us!"

A chorus of agreement confirmed it. Women were behind every bush, tree, and outbuilding. One had climbed onto the roof of the barn for a better shot.

"This is my farm and we will do as I say," Patrice silenced them. "I was hasty in ordering you to open fire before. I won't make the same mistake twice. Argent is too important. She is the one person who was not afraid to point the finger of blame where it belongs when all the rest of us were too scared to speak up, and she has backed us all the way since."

Backed them or helped make things worse? Fargo asked himself, a sentiment he chose not to share.

"So which of you would rather she stay in there?" Patrice asked. When none of the other women replied, she said, "I didn't think so." She turned to the house. "What have you decided, mister? I'd take advantage of my offer, were I you, before I change my mind."

Fargo looked at Clover. "I'll leave it up to you." Although he had ridden in determined to bring the war to an end, he would not do it at the cost of innocent lives. The women were not to blame for the war. Nor, for that matter, were the men. Both sides were being manipulated. Although to what end, only the rider on the bay knew.

"I'd as soon stand and fight," Clover said, "but it would serve no purpose. So I reckon we might as well accept."

Smothering his disappointment at how it had turned out, Fargo rose. "All right! Here we come."

"Not so fast," Patrice said. "Send Argent out first. After I see she's fine, you can be on your way."

As luck would have it, at that exact moment the schoolteacher groaned and slowly sat up, rubbing her jaw. "You hit me," she glowered at Fargo.

"I tapped you," Fargo rubbed in the insult. Stepping to the door, he opened it, but did not show himself. "Out you go. Patrice has agreed to let us leave if we hand you over to her unhurt."

"She's done what?" Argent pushed to her feet. With her squat body, light mustache, and short hair, she was unlike any schoolmarm Fargo ever met. "Well then, we shouldn't keep her waiting, should we?" She squared her shoulders and marched outside. As she passed Fargo, she said so only he could hear, "How does it feel to go through life as dumb as a tree stump?"

Before Fargo could respond, Argent dashed across the yard. Most of the women came from hiding to happily flock about her, some clapping her on the back. Patrice joined them, and Argent and she immediately became embroiled in a heated spat. Fargo could not catch all they said because they were keeping their voices low, but he overheard Patrice saying she had given her word, and Argent retorting that giving one's word to a traitor and a killer was no word at all.

"What's happenin'?" Clover was beside him. "Why is it takin' so long?"

"Never trust a schoolmarm," Fargo said.

The women formed a skirmish line. Argent, smirking smugly, put a hand to her mouth. "Guess what, mister? The ladies have had a change of heart. You're not going anywhere. Unless you count six feet under."

"Patrice gave her word!" Clover cried. "We held up our end. Now you hold up yours."

"Patrice made the deal, not me," Argent said. "I'm under no obligation to honor it. And in case you haven't noticed, what I say goes. So throw out your guns and come out with your hands up."

"Go to hell," Fargo summed up his feelings, and closed the door.

Argent did not waste an instant. "Open fire!" Once more rifles and pistols boomed and cracked as Fargo took hold of Clover's hand and darted behind the settee. The air swarmed with leaden bees; slugs struck the mantle, shattered the clock, sent bits of wood flying from the walls and furniture.

Fargo dropped prone, Clover's body glued to his, and he could tell she was afraid but trying mightily not to show it.

There came a lull, but it was all too brief. "Reload, sisters!" Argent bawled. "Reload and have at them again!"

Fargo was tired of being a sitting target. Patting Clover's shoulder, he slid to the window. Few of the women had sought cover. He sighted on one who was feeding a cartridge into a rifle, at a point high on her right shoulder. But then, as he was about to squeeze the trigger, he lowered the barrel and fired into the ground at their feet, four rapid shots that scattered the whole bunch like hens fleeing a fox. They ran every which way, some bumping into one another in their haste.

"Look at them scoot," Clover giggled. She had crawled up beside him.

"High and mighty Argent, too. She's no braver than anyone else when it comes right down to it."

"You should take cover," Fargo advised.

"Hill folk stand by their friends," Clover said. "Besides, I'm no sissified city gal who's afraid to fire a gun."

"Come on, then." Fargo hurried down the hall to a room on the left. The window had been shot out and pieces of glass covered the hardwood floor. They crunched under his boots as he crossed to the other side, and hunkered. Two women were by a shed to the northeast, another was behind a tree to the northwest. The Ovaro was twenty yards beyond the tree, standing quietly. The stallion had grown accustomed to gunfire over the years and seldom spooked anymore.

"You plan to make a dash for your horse?" Clover guessed.

"Unless you have a better idea." Fargo could keep the pair at the shed pinned down. The woman by the tree, however, posed a problem. To reach the Ovaro they had to go right past her. If she stood her ground, he would have no recourse but to shoot her. He raised the Henry.

"That's Mildred," Clover said. "She just turned twenty last month. You should hear her sing. She has the voice of an angel."

Fargo lowered the Henry, and swore.

"Something wrong?"

"Somewhere or other I picked up a conscience and it's been aggravating the hell out of me ever since," Fargo confided.

Clover touched his cheek. "Don't be so hard on yourself. I think it's sweet, you havin' a heart of gold."

Fargo wouldn't go that far. But he did have his own set of scruples, a personal code he lived by; he never took a life except in self-defense, he never lied except when he had to, and he never cheated at cards unless someone else was cheating.

"I'll go first," Clover offered. "Mildred is less likely to shoot me than she is you." Clover went to sidle past.

"Not yet." Fargo said. Riders had abruptly appeared approximately a mile away. Eight, nine, ten in all, from wooded hills bordering the valley to the north. They were too far off to identify. As he watched, they started toward the farmhouse at a gallop. He was so intent on them that he almost missed spotting another group of ten riders a quarter-mile to the east of the first group. "What do you make of that?" he asked.

Clover rose in a crouch and promptly dropped down again when a rifle spat smoke and lead and part of the windowsill exploded in fragments.

"Careful or you'll get your head blown off," Fargo cautioned. He backed toward the doorway. "Come on. I have a better idea."

The stairs to the second floor were near the kitchen. Fargo climbed two at a stride and entered an upstairs bedroom. The windows here were intact. Moving as close as he dared, he stared at the oncoming riders.

"There's another bunch!" Clover exclaimed.

A third group was to the west. Like the others, they were spreading out, and it was plain that by the time they reached the farmhouse they would have it encircled on three sides. Fargo wondered if there were more riders to the south. Hastening into a bedroom across the way, he confirmed his hunch.

"I don't like the looks of this," was Clover's assessment.

Neither did Fargo. By now the beards of many of the riders were all too apparent. "We couldn't leave now if Argent let us."

"There's Bramwell! And Porter!" In her anxiety, Clover stepped in front of the window. "It's come! The moment we've always dreaded! Every last man in our clan must be out there."

"Are you trying to get yourself killed?" Fargo asked as he pulled her to one side. Fortunately, none of the women had spotted her.

"We've got to warn Patrice and the others," Clover urged. "They don't even realize it yet." Wresting her arm free, she bent down and undid the latch and raised the window as high as it would go.

Fargo yanked on her shirt just as a shot rang out. A slug cleaved the space she had occupied and struck the far wall. "Damn it. Stay down."

"Don't you understand?" Clover pushed at his chest. "Porter is at the end of his patience! It's the showdown we've all long dreaded!"

The riders were slowing. Rifles were shucked from scabbards and revolvers were flourished.

"See?" Clover sought to reach the stairs but Fargo would not release his hold. "Let me go!" she pleaded. "If I don't get down there, the women will be wiped out."

"It won't come to that." Fargo was fairly confident that once the two sides met face-to-face and talked it over, bloodshed could be averted. Provided he was down there to talk some sense into them.

Suddenly there was a wild shout. The women had noticed the men. Simultaneously, the valley rocked to the thunder of fifty guns.

17

Whirling, Fargo ran down the hall to a bedroom at the front of the house and over to a window. The men had the farmhouse ringed and were slowly advancing, gun smoke curling from the ends of many of their rifles and pistol barrels. They had fired into the air, not at the women, and the reason became clear when Porter Jackson smirked and hollered, "Did that get your attention, ladies?"

Startled women were backing toward the house, their weapons pointed at their menfolk. Few appeared eager to start a general bloodbath.

Porter Jackson, his son Bramwell, and his grandson Samuel, rode three abreast. Elders were conspicuous by their gray beards. But a lot of younger men were present. Maybe every man in the clan.

Argent Meriwether and Patrice were shoulder to shoulder, flanked by a dozen of their followers. They halted and Argent bawled, "That's close enough, old man! Keep them back or you will regret it!"

Porter kept on coming, his voice thick with scorn. "What you want, outsider, is of no consequence. Your days of deceivin' my people are over."

Bramwell brandished his rifle. "Let me shoot her, Pa, and get this over with."

The threat goaded Patrice into stepping in front of the teacher. "If you do, cousin, you will have to kill me first, and the rest of us as well. She is under our protection."

When Porter drew rein, the men came to a stop. Nerves were razor taut. Fingers were poised on triggers and hammers.

"Oh God," Clover whispered. "What do we do?"

"What *can* we do?" Fargo rejoined. If he poked his head out, it would be shot off. Both sides wanted him dead and were not about to listen to anything he had to say.

Porter had placed his rifle across his saddle and now leaned on his saddle horn. "Patrice, I don't mind tellin' you that you are a severe disappointment. I expected better of my middle son's wife. Joe would roll over in his grave if he knew how you turned on those who care for you most."

"How do you know he's dead," Patrice asked, "unless you're the one who killed him?"

"Be sensible, woman," Porter said harshly. "Do you really believe I would murder the fruit of my own loins? I know Joseph is dead because it's the only explanation for him going missin'. He loved you, loved your kids, loved his kin and these mountains. He would never up and leave without tellin' someone."

Fargo could not see Patrice's face but he sensed that the patriarch's words had an effect. Her rigid spine relaxed and she lowered her rifle and took a half step toward him.

"I figured the same thing, but with everything else that has gone on, you can't blame me for suspectin' you were behind it."

For a sterling moment the two sides were on the verge of being reconciled. Then Argent Meriwether grabbed Patrice and spun her around. "Surely you're not gullible enough to fall for his vile lies? Have you forgotten how he treated you after your daughter was killed? Have you forgotten all your sisters who have given their lives for the cause?"

"Hush up, witch," Porter snapped. "You've caused enough trouble."

"Me?" Argent snarled. "You're the one who threatened Patrice when she stood up to you and said Elly was too young to be given away in marriage. You were the one who told me that you would see me dead rather than let me spread my venom, as you called it."

It was young Samuel, not Porter, who responded. "Please, Miss Meriwether, can't we all be reasonable for once? You're surrounded and outnumbered. This is not the time to make people madder than they already are."

"This is the perfect time!" Argent cried. "It was bound to come to this sooner or later, so let's get it over with."

"Want to end this, do you?" Porter said. "Then lay down your rifle and submit to being placed in custody."

"You have no authority over me, old man," Argent fed his anger. "Or the women here with me. Take your bootlicking offspring and leave while you still can."

Porter transformed to stone, a crimson tinge rising from his neck to his hairline. "Did you hear her, kinsmen? Did you hear this wretched excuse for a human being? This uppity outsider who thinks she knows better than we do how we should live? Who has meddled and carped and twisted the truth until we've been at each other's throats like rabid dogs?" He rose in his stirrups and scanned the line of horsemen. "We can't tolerate her another day. Another minute. We must end this travesty here and now. And the best way to cure a cancer is to cut it out." Jerking his rifle to his shoulder, Porter aimed at Argent and fired.

Whether it was his sudden movement or some other cause, Samuel's horse unexpectedly shied. It wheeled to the left, or tried to, and collided with Porter's mount, jarring Porter so that the rifle barrel dipped and the shot intended for Argent dug a furrow in the earth between her feet.

"Into the house, Sisters!" Meriwether bawled, and squeezed off a shot of her own. An elder next to Bramwell clutched at his chest and toppled.

Mayhem ensued. Lead flew thick and furious. Men fell from horses. Women sprawled to the dirt. But not everyone, Fargo saw, joined in the wild melee. Some on both sides refused to join in, the blood in their veins counting for more than the anger in their hearts.

Samuel's was not the only horse to act up. Other mounts reared and panicked and tried to flee, only to be reined back around into the heat of the fray by the incensed men astride them.

And all the while, Argent and Patrice and the rest of the women were backing into the house, firing as they went. In no time at all, thick, choking clouds of gun smoke shrouded the yard and the men, and the shooting dwindled.

Fargo heard shoes clomp on the floorboards below, heard the front and back doors slam shut, and the hubbub of dozens of women and children speaking all at once. Motioning to Clover, he crept to the head of the stairs but did not descend. For the moment Argent and the others had forgotten they were there and he wanted to keep it that way.

"Calm down!" Patrice was shouting. "Everyone stay calm and we'll be fine!"

Evangeline did not share her outlook. "Why did Argent have to shoot Elder Zebulon? Now the men will want our hides."

Her criticism rankled Argent. "When will you get it through your head, Sister Evangeline, that the men are your enemies? That it's kill or be killed? That you should not be standing there making wild accusations but over at a window, shooting those who would gladly shoot you?"

Fargo descended several steps and craned his neck over the bannister. Eight or nine women were clustered around Argent and Patrice. One with gray streaks in her hair cleared her throat.

"Those are our fathers, our husbands, our brothers and cousins. They won't harm us if we lay down our weapons and surrender."

"You would give up after all we have been through?" Argent asked, incredulous. "You can forget Elly? Forget all the others who have died? Forget how downtrodden you were before you saw the light of modern ways?"

"I'm sorry about Elly and the others," the woman said, "but I don't believe the men had a hand in it. As for that downtrodden stuff, all I know is that before you came along, I was as happy as a flea in a doghouse. Now I'm sad as can be, and growin' sadder by the day."

"Same here," someone chimed in.

Argent bared her teeth like a wolf at bay and savagely gestured at the front door. "Go ahead, then. Walk out there and see what happens. I can guarantee they won't let you take two steps."

Everyone looked at the middle-aged woman. She shoved her rifle at another, marched to the door, and worked the latch. But she had barely begun to pull when a rifle cracked twice and two holes appeared in the door inches above her head. Frightened, she ducked down.

"See?" Argent crowed. "I told you! Now will you forget about throwing your life away and help us in our cause?"

Whoever fired the shots unwittingly firmed the rebels' resolve. Their faces grim, the women moved to the windows and down the hall to other rooms. Fargo was caught off guard and had no time to bound back up the stairs, but no one glanced in his direction.

Soon only Argent and Patrice were near the door.

Argent beckoned, and they moved toward the sitting room.

Turning, Fargo began to take a step but he bumped into Clover, who once again had come up close behind him. She was balanced on the balls of her feet on the edge of the step above so she could see over his shoulder, and when they collided, she grabbed him to keep from falling. In so doing, she dropped her rifle.

The *thunk* of the butt striking the stairs was loud enough to be heard halfway down the hallway, but it was nothing compared to the blast of the rifle when it discharged.

Fargo tried to grab it but it clattered to the bottom.

"What the hell?" Argent Meriwether barreled toward the stairs.

An arm around Clover, Fargo sprang to the top, and crouched. A shadow appeared. Then another. A hand thrust out and snatched Clover's rifle. A foot rose toward the first step.

To discourage them, Fargo fired into the floor.

The foot disappeared and Patrice shouted, "Stay back! He can pick us off easy from up there!"

Whispering ensued, and Argent yelled up, "You have the advantage at the moment, mister. We can't come up because killing you isn't worth the cost. But you can't come down, either. Not unless you and the betrayer want to be riddled with more holes than a sieve."

"Patrice?" Clover yelled. "Don't listen to her. I've always been your friend, haven't I? Believe me when I tell you the men aren't to blame for this stupid war. Talk to them. Go out under a white flag and hear their side."

"Oh sure," Patrice replied. "And be shot dead like they almost shot Martha a minute ago? No thanks."

More whispering ended with Argent bellowing, "Remember, we have the stairs covered. Don't meddle and you'll live longer."

Clover had the panicked expression of a trapped animal. "We're boxed in."

That they were, Fargo reflected. Going out a window would be suicide; the men would gun them down the moment they showed themselves.

A shout from outside resulted in a rush toward the front of the house. Fargo nodded at Clover and they hastened to the window facing the front yard.

Most of the men had dismounted. Porter had his hands on his hips and was impatiently rocking back and forth on his heels. "Patrice Jackson! I would have words with you! Step outside if you have the grit."

The front door must have opened because Patrice said, "This is as far as I'll come. I don't trust you. Nor any of those with you."

"Tell that to Elder Zebulon, lyin' dead yonder. Or to the other three men who have breathed their last this day due to your childish female folly."

"Some of us were shot too," Patrice said coldly.

"Serves you right! Your side started it!" Porter fumed. "This bloodlettin' is on your head, not mine! As it has been all along! You and that abomination of womanhood you've harbored!"

"What about the women *you've* killed?" Patrice railed. "Your soul is no cleaner than mine!"

"Again you're talkin' nonsense. I haven't killed anyone. My knife was planted near Billy and Elly."

"Liar!"

A shouting match would get them nowhere except lead to more slaughter. There had to be a way to end the madness before the Jacksons wiped themselves out. Squatting, Fargo opened the window just enough to yell down, "Porter! Bramwell! Listen to me! The women aren't to blame."

Porter jerked up his rifle but didn't fire. "You! What are you doing here?" Bramwell said something Fargo couldn't hear, and Porter nodded. "As I've been sayin' all along, you're in league with these biddies. How much are they payin' you to do their dirty work?"

Patrice answered him before Fargo could. "He's not on our side. He's on yours. Don't pretend different."

"Who's pretendin', you silly female?" Porter growled. "You know how I feel about outsiders. It was bad enough we had to hire the schoolmarm. Do you honestly think I would have that yokel in buckskins do my fightin' for me?"

"Yokel?" Fargo said.

"No, I don't," Patrice had answered. "You've always said the clan should handle its own problems. That outsiders bring nothin' but trouble and we should shun them like they have the plague."

"I haven't changed my outlook any, I can tell you that," Porter declared.

Argent must have shown herself because Porter's face clouded with raw hate and he demanded, "What do you want, you hideous bitch? I didn't ask you to take part. Go back inside."

"I won't let you bend these women to your will with your lies and intimidation," was Argent's rebuttal.

"What the hell are you babblin' about?" Porter snapped. "I never lie. And I might be stern at times but only for the good of the clan." He dismissed her with a gesture. "This is Jackson business. Get out of my sight."

"Do as he wants, Sister Argent," Patrice said. "He and I are finally talkin' things out. Maybe the worst is over."

"*I* say when it's over, not this devious murdering bastard. Here's what I think of him and his kind."

The blast of Argent's rifle riveted the men in astonishment. Bramwell's mouth fell open and he gawked in horror as his father folded at the knees and oozed to the grass like a gob of hot wax oozing down a candle. No one moved, no one spoke.

"Did you see?" Bramwell found his voice, and jammed his rifle to his shoulder. "Kill them! Kill every last one!"

Above the thunderous blast of gunfire keened the scream of a terror-struck child.

18

The girl's cry sent Fargo racing down the hall to the top of the stairs. He slowed just long enough to verify he had a round in the Henry's chamber, and then he went down the steps three at a bound.

Two women were at the bottom standing guard but they were facing the front of the house and did not hear him until he was right on top of them. One spun, jerking her rifle up, and Fargo slammed the Henry's stock against her temple. The other leaped back and brought up a pistol. She was fast, but not faster than Fargo, who darted in close and delivered an uppercut that left her lying next to her companion.

A battle raged. The weeks of boiling hatred and misunderstanding had spilled over into rampant violence. Many of the women were at windows, returning fire. Others reloaded. Others wanted no part of the madness and huddled in corners or behind furniture. The children were cowering in the kitchen, two older women trying to prevent hysterics.

Patrice and Argent Meriwether had made it back inside but Patrice was leaning against a wall, her left hand over a spreading red stain on her right arm. From the unnatural angle at which her arm was bent, the bone was broken.

Argent was bellowing commands like an army general. "Stay low! Aim for their chests! That way if you miss their hearts, you'll still hit something!"

A woman at a front window was flung back, her face a red smear.

Clover tugged on Fargo's sleeve and rose onto her toes to shout in his ear, "We have to stop this!"

That they did, and Fargo knew exactly how he was going to go about it. He stalked toward Meriwether and saw a woman of twenty or so on her knees, clutching her bosom and sobbing, "This is wrong! This is wrong! This is so wrong!" A woman at a window on his right cried out and fell. Another was wounded in the hip. The clan was being decimated by their own pigheadedness.

Fargo was only a few yards from the schoolteacher's broad back when Evangeline materialized out of the gun smoke and came near to plowing into him. She had a Colt, *his* Colt, and she was hastily reloading.

"You!"

"Me," Fargo said, and grabbing the barrel, he tore the revolver from her grasp and slammed the butt against her chin. Once again he could not bring himself to use all his strength for fear he would break her jaw and crush her teeth. But the blow left her on her back, moaning and quaking, and that was enough.

Argent was in the middle of the front room. She did not seem to care that a steady stream of lead sizzled by her. "That's it!" she encouraged her followers. "Don't stop! We want them all dead! Dead! Dead! Dead!"

Suddenly Clover screeched, "Skye! Behind you!"

Fargo spun. Patrice had raised her rifle to shoot him in the back but she could not hold it steady enough with only one arm. Grimacing in torment, tears filling her eyes, she let it drop and began crying.

Clover ran to her.

A tremendous blow jarred the door on its hinges. The men were attempting to batter it down. "Again, men! Again!" Bramwell's voice rose above the din, urging them on.

Fargo turned and locked eyes with Argent Meriwether. Hers were fiery pools of blazing hatred. A hate so intense, it dominated every fiber of her being. Her face had a maniacal sheen, her lips were pulled back from her teeth in a feral snarl. She seemed more animal than human.

"I won't let you stop me!"

Too late, Fargo realized she had a revolver pointed at him, and that she had the hammer thumbed back. He dived to the right as her trigger finger tightened, but instead of a shot and a spurt of gun smoke, there was a faint click. He charged her as she squeezed the trigger again and yet a third time. For once, though, luck was with him—the cylinder was empty.

Fargo was only a few steps from her when Argent hissed and threw the revolver at his face. He ducked, then had to sidestep to spare his groin from a vicious kick. Her hands sought his throat, her fingers gouging deep. *God, she is strong!* Fargo thought, as he let the Henry and the Colt fall and seized her wrists. He pulled with all his might but her fingers only dug in deeper, choking off his breath and threatening to rip out his throat by sheer brutish strength.

"You and your damned meddling!" Argent raged, spittle flecking her lips. "You'll spoil my revenge!"

Fargo swung her to the right and then to the left but he could not shake her off. He drove a knee into her gut but it had no effect. Her insane hatred had infused her limbs with inhuman strength. Her fingers were iron stakes. He punched and pried and gasped for air that wasn't there.

Then her mouth yawned wide and with a bestial howl Argent sought to bury her teeth in his neck. Fargo strained to keep her from succeeding. In their thrashing and struggling he backed against the rear wall and had nowhere to go. It enabled her to plant her legs so she could not be moved. Her teeth edged slowly but inexorably toward his jugular.

Fargo's lungs were aching; he was close to blacking out. But he refused to give up. He refused to be beaten. Not by her, not by anyone. Again and again he smashed his fist into her face, a succession of punches that weakened her grip and her stance but were not enough to break her hold. She was bleeding from her nose and her mouth and she had a knot over one eye but still she clung on. Still she tried to throttle the life from him.

Raising both arms over his head, Fargo cupped his hands and brought them crashing down, clubbing her again and again and again. With each blow her grip loosened a little more. But even as her knees folded, she clung to him by force of will.

Covered with blood, battered and swollen, Argent looked up at him with undimmed hatred. "I should have shot you on sight!"

"The feeling is mutual," Fargo said, and clubbed her a final time. She collapsed at his feet and he leaned back against the wall. It felt as if a grizzly had chewed on his throat and a lance had been driven through his lungs. But he could not stand there and suffer. The battle still raged, as he was reminded when a wild slug bit slivers from the wall next to him.

Forcing his legs to move, Fargo retrieved his guns. Argent was sitting up when he pressed the Henry's muzzle to her head. "That's far enough."

Some of the women were reloading and the shooting outside had briefly tapered. In the lull Fargo shouted, "Not one more shot or she dies!"

Eleven women were in the sitting room, more in the room directly across from it. Several, like Patrice, were wounded. The rest were tired and scared, and Fargo could tell their hearts were no longer in it. They were sick of the fighting, sick of the bloodshed. "Lay down your guns!"

"But the men—" Prudence protested. Her hair was disheveled, her face streaked with grime.

"I won't let them hurt you," Fargo promised.

As if to put him to the test, the front door splintered to the battering impact of a fence rail the men had torn from the corral and into the house rushed Bramwell and others. They stopped in surprise at the sight before them, Bramwell's brow furrowing in confusion. "What is this? You're not on their side like Pa thought?"

"How many times must I tell you, you lunkhead," Fargo said in exasperation. "I'm not on *anyone's* side."

Bramwell grinned with vengeful glee at Meriwether. "You did right fine, mister. Now step aside and let us finish it."

"No."

Stopping cold, Bramwell fingered his rifle. "What the hell do you mean, no? That bitch shot my pa. If you think she's leavin' here alive, you've got another think comin'."

"Don't you want to know what this was really all about?" Fargo responded.

Bramwell's confusion climbed. "You're makin' no sense. We all know it started when the women blamed Pa for murderin' Elly and Billy, and he did no such thing."

"What if the women aren't to blame, either?"

"Now you're talkin' in circles," Bramwell said. "If it wasn't the men and it wasn't the women, then who—" He blinked at Argent Meriwether. "God Almighty! It was right in front of our noses the whole time."

Argent was conscious. She slowly sat up and spat blood onto the floor. "You think you have it figured out but you don't." A grin curled her ruin of a mouth as red drops dribbled between her broken teeth and down over her pulped lower lip.

"Who else if it wasn't one of us?" Bramwell pointed

at Fargo. "It couldn't be him. He didn't show up until long after it began."

"It's not the *who* that matters," Argent rasped. "It's the *why*."

"I don't understand," Bramwell said.

"Of course you don't," Argent spat. "You're a jackass. An ignorant lout, like the rest of the Jackson men. And the women aren't any better. Stupid as cows, the whole bunch."

"What was that?" Patrice said, coming closer.

Argent tittered, a high-pitched laugh that did not sound entirely sane. "I fooled you all! Fooled every last one of you miserable murdering vermin! If not for him"—Argent bobbed her bloody chin at Fargo—"I'd have done it. I'd have wiped the Jackson clan off the face of the earth." Her laugh swelled to a shriek of demented joy. "Or, to be more precise, you would have done it for me."

Fargo stepped back and lowered the Henry. He had an inkling where this was leading, even if the others didn't.

"Why would you do such a thing?" Clover asked. "We never did you any harm."

"Didn't you?" Argent said, and then screeched, *"Didn't you?"* She tried to stand but she could not rise higher than her knees. She shook a thick finger at them, at all of them, one after the other, and as she did, she cackled. "Look at your stupid faces! You still don't have any idea. You still don't realize who I am."

"You're a teacher from Philadelphia," Bramwell said.

"But that's not where I was born and raised," Argent revealed. Suddenly her voice changed. It acquired a Southern twang that made Fargo think of the hill folk of the Deep South, from states like Alabama or Georgia—or North Carolina. "How you ever beat my kin I will never know."

Shock registered. Some of the Jacksons had divined the truth. Not Bramwell, though. As confused as ever, he said quizzically, "Your kin?"

"Yes, you brainless lump." Argent was shaking as she spoke but not from pain. "My father and my uncles and my cousins! People I cared most for in this world! People I loved!" Rage brought her to her feet. "I can see I'll have to spell it out for you. Meriwether is my married name. My maiden name was Harker." She paused. "Argenta Harker."

They had it, then, every last one.

"My pa was Zechariah Harker, head of our clan." Argent took a faltering step toward Bramwell. "It was *your* pa who tricked him by saying he wanted to end the feud, and when my pa showed up at the meeting place, your pa took him prisoner. It was *your* pa who sent word to the men in our clan that if they wanted to see my pa alive, they were to come to Smokey Hollow. It was *your* pa who set up the ambush that killed nearly every last male Harker." She reached Bramwell and poked him in the chest. "Your father was a butcher and you're no better!"

Bramwell was too stunned to reply.

"When the agency wrote me that Jacksonville was looking to hire a schoolmarm, I couldn't wait to get here. I'd wanted a position further west but I never dreamed things would work out as they did. Here I was, the one person who hated you most in this world, free to walk among you and do as I pleased. Free to repay you for nearly wiping out my clan by wiping out yours."

"So it *was* you who killed Elly and Billy!" Bramwell declared.

"No, Pa, it was me."

Everyone turned toward the south window. The glass had been shot out, and the curtains were lying on the floor, shot to pieces. Just outside stood the man in black, his hat brim pulled low, a bandanna covering the lower half of his face. Only now he reached up and pulled the bandanna down around his neck. When his hands rose into sight again, each held a revolver.

"Samuel?" Bramwell blurted, going white as a sheet. "This can't be."

"But it is, Pa," Sam said. "I'm in love with her. She promised she would go away with me if I did as she wanted. I helped her knife Elly and Billy. Ever since, we've taken turns doing the killin'. And you know what? After the first two, the rest were easy." He gazed lovingly at Argenta. "I would do anything for her, anything at all."

Total shock set in. The Jacksons were statues, unwilling to believe the evidence of their own eyes.

Argenta broke the spell by laughing and saying, "It was easy wrapping that fool boy around my finger. All I had to do was pull down his britches and he would walk on hot coals for me. The fool."

"What?" Sam said.

That was when Patrice walked over and raised the muzzle of her rifle close to Argenta's chin and squeezed the trigger. The slug burst out the top of Argenta's head, showering brains and bone and gore on those who were nearest.

"No!" Sam cried, and fired from the hip. His shot entered Patrice low on her ribs and exited under her other arm. She died without a sound, falling across the body of the woman she had just slain.

Evangeline aimed her rifle but Sam shot her through the chest and then an elder jerked his rifle up but Sam shot him too, and then it was Bramwell who took aim but he hesitated, choked with emotion, and said plaintively, "How could you?"

"I loved her," Sam said, and thumbed back a hammer.

Fargo fired, heard the fleshy splat of lead, fired again as Sam swivelled toward him, fired a third time as Sam fired but Sam's bullet went into the floor and his spun Sam around and wilted the stripling like a flower too long under a scorching sun. Sam pitched across the sill, his arms limp, his revolvers falling from lifeless fingers.

"No," Bramwell said. "No, no, no."

Fargo picked up the Henry and was out the door before anyone could think to stop him. He was halfway to the Ovaro when Clover caught up.

"You're leavin'? Just like that?"

"Sorry," Fargo said, and kissed her on the cheek. "Maybe we'll see each other again one day." But that was unlikely since he would never, ever come anywhere near Jacksonville for as long as he lived. Mounting, he spurred the Ovaro to a trot. He looked back to be sure no one was after him. Clover waved and he returned it. Then he faced west and breathed deep of the wind on his face and in his hair, and he did not look back again.

LOOKING FORWARD!
**The following is the opening
section from the next novel in the exciting
Trailsman series from Signet:**

THE TRAILSMAN #276

SKELETON CANYON

*Arizona, 1860—A rich, wild land where evil
men cast long shadows in the hot sun.*

The big man in buckskins was coated with a thick
layer of trail dust, as was the black-and-white Ovaro
stallion he led along the street. Weariness lay heavily
on both of them, but no amount of exhaustion could
completely disguise the strength and vigor that was
naturally theirs. Man and horse were both magnificent
specimens, and under better circumstances that would
be evident.

But right now they were plumb worn out after days
on a long, hard trail, and all they wanted was rest.

The man, at least, was not destined to get it. Not
right away, anyway.

His name was Skye Fargo. At the sound of a loud,

angry voice, he raised his head and looked to the left, toward a saloon called the Pine Tree. A man came flying backwards through the entrance, knocking aside the batwing doors. His booted feet flailed desperately as he tried to catch his balance on the wide boardwalk, but he failed in the effort and plunged off the edge into the street, to land with a resounding crash right in front of Fargo.

Fargo stopped and looked down at the man, as did the stallion. Fargo's gaze was one of curiosity, because his mind was always alert no matter how tired he was. The Ovaro, on the other hand, regarded the man lying in the dust with more of a baleful glare. This human, whoever he was, formed a barrier between the horse and its rightful rest.

The man on the ground blinked rheumy eyes, stared up at Fargo, and said, "Lord, you're a big one, ain't you?"

"Are you all right, old-timer?" Fargo asked.

The man, who was mostly bald, with a fringe of white hair that matched his tuft of white beard, pushed himself unsteadily to his feet. His leathery face showed the effects of years spent in sun and wind, in biting cold and blistering heat. His clothes were on the ragged side, but not too tattered. He swatted at them, raising clouds of dust, and said, "I'm fine, lad, don't worry about me."

He had a slight accent, probably British, Fargo thought. He had run into Englishmen on the frontier before. This big land drew all sorts, from all over the world.

Fargo slapped the man on the shoulder and started to lead the stallion around him. "All right, then. Better be more careful in the future."

"Oh, I intend to. No more fisticuffs for me." The

old man turned toward the Pine Tree Saloon, and as he did so, he reached into the front of his shirt and pulled a gun that had been tucked into the waistband of his ragged trousers.

Fargo's lake-blue eyes narrowed. From the looks of it, the old-timer intended to burst back into the saloon and start blazing away at whomever had thrown him out. As Fargo got a better look at the gun in the light that spilled through the saloon's entrance, he revised his opinion. The revolver was ancient and rusted, and probably wouldn't fire.

But if the old man stomped in there and started waving it around, odds were that somebody would pull a working gun and let some daylight into his innards. Other people might get hit by stray bullets if lead started flying, too.

So even though this was really none of his business, Fargo sighed, reached out, and caught hold of the old man's sleeve.

"Wait a minute," Fargo said. "You don't want to go in there like that."

"The hell I don't." The old man tried unsuccessfully to tug his sleeve loose from Fargo's grip. "A feller's got to defend his honor, don't you know?"

"Getting killed is no way to do it."

The old-timer turned an owlish gaze toward Fargo. "Sometimes it's the only way," he said softly.

Fargo might have continued the argument, but at that moment, heavy footsteps from the boardwalk made him glance in that direction. A tall, massively built man with broad shoulders and long arms seemingly as thick as tree trunks had slapped the batwings open and stepped out of the saloon. He had an ugly, rawboned face and a tangle of coppery hair under a pushed-back black hat. He hooked his thumbs in the gunbelt strapped around his hips and said, "How come you're just standin' there, you damned old pelican? Didn't I tell you to drag your ass outta Gila City?"

The old man's eyes widened even more. He started to jerk the useless old revolver upward, but he was slow about it, more than slow enough to get himself killed. The man on the boardwalk cursed and grabbed for his own iron.

Fargo left his feet in a flying tackle.

He crashed into the old man and bore him to the ground as a gun roared. The slug spanked through the space where the old-timer's head had been a split second earlier. Fargo rolled over and surged up into a crouch. He held his left hand toward the man on the boardwalk, palm out, as he shouted, "Hold your fire!" His right hand hovered close to the butt of the Colt on his hip just in case the man tried to trigger another shot.

The man on the boardwalk let the barrel of his gun drop a little. Smoke curled from the muzzle. "What in blue blazes are you doin', mister?" he yelled at Fargo. "You could'a got yourself killed!"

"Nobody needs to get killed over this," Fargo said. "Just take it easy."

The man on the boardwalk snorted in contempt. "Tell that to that worthless old bum whose hide you just saved. He's the one who pulled iron on me."

Fargo reached down and picked up the revolver the old man had dropped. "You couldn't hammer a nail with this thing without it falling apart, let alone shoot anybody."

"Well, how in hell was I supposed to know that? All I saw was somebody tryin' to point a gun at me!"

The man had a point, Fargo thought. The old-timer was at least partially to blame for this ruckus.

"All right, you know now you don't have anything

to worry about. Why don't you holster that hogleg and go back inside?"

"You gonna get that stinkin' old man out of here?"

"If that's what it takes," Fargo said.

The man shrugged and slid his gun back in its holster. "All right. But if I catch sight of him again tonight, I'm liable to beat him to death. Remember that."

Fargo didn't say anything, but he didn't think he was likely to forget the big redheaded man—or his threats.

The man went back into the Pine Tree. The rest of the saloon's patrons had crowded around the door and the windows, watching the confrontation, and they greeted him with cheers and backslaps as if he were some sort of conquering hero. Fargo just shook his head and reached down to help the old-timer to his feet.

"You didn't have to do that," the old man whined. "I don't need nobody to fight my battles."

"Then you should choose them more wisely," Fargo said. He picked up his wide-brimmed brown hat, which had fallen off when he tackled the old man, slapped it against his thigh to get some of the dust off it, and put it back on his head. He wrapped his fingers around the old man's skinny upper arm. "Come on. You look like you could use something to eat, and so could I."

Actually, when he had reached Gila City, he had been thinking more of sleep than anything else, but he was willing to postpone that for a while. He steered the old man down the settlement's main street and a couple of blocks later found a hole-in-the-wall hash house that was still open. Fargo left the Ovaro at the hitch rail and took the old man inside.

The place had no tables, only crude stools along a

counter made of rough-hewn planks. Fargo and the old man were the only customers. The proprietor was a middle-aged Chinese man who put burned steaks and scorched potatoes in front of Fargo and the old-timer without asking what they wanted, then added cups of steaming coffee. The food was pretty bad, but Fargo was hungry enough to eat it anyway. The coffee was a different story. In one of those rare instances of finding a diamond surrounded by trash, it was wonderful. Fargo felt some of his strength returning as he sipped the strong black brew.

"I appreciate this, lad," the old-timer said as he gnawed at the tough steak. "Things have been a bit lean and hungry in recent weeks." He put his fork down and extended a gnarled hand. "Bert Olmsted," he introduced himself.

Fargo shook with him. "Skye Fargo."

"It's pleased I am to make your acquaintance, Mr. Fargo. Or should I call you Skye?"

Fargo shrugged. "Whatever you like."

"Call you anything as long as it's not late to supper, eh?" Bert Olmsted slapped the counter and cackled. "You Yanks and your witticisms."

Fargo wasn't the one who had made the weak joke, but he let that pass. Olmsted might not be falling-down drunk, but it was obvious he had put away a considerable amount of Who-hit-John during the evening. Fargo thought the food and coffee might sober him up a little.

"Who was that fella who tossed you out of the Pine Tree?" Fargo asked when they had polished off the steak and potatoes.

"The Miscreant's name is Flynn Pearsoll," Olmsted replied. "And a more belligerent sort I've never run across. All I did was ask him to perhaps stand me the cost of a drink, and he acted like a bull seeing red.

Bellowed that I stank and threw me bodily out of the establishment." Olmsted sniffed. "I suppose I am a bit odiferous, but still, there are limits."

"You shouldn't have pulled your gun."

"Yes, I suppose you're correct about that. By the way, might I have it back?"

Fargo had tucked the old revolver behind his belt. He took it out and slid it along the counter to Olmsted. "Is that thing even loaded?"

"Of course. What good is an unloaded gun?"

In this case, it probably didn't matter, but there was always a slight chance that the revolver might go off if it was loaded. "Better be careful with it," Fargo said. "It looks like it might blow up on you if you tried to fire it."

"Nonsense. It's a fine weapon." Olmsted looked Fargo up and down. "You're rather heavily armed yourself, my friend."

Fargo had the Colt on his hip and an Arkansas Toothpick in a fringed sheath strapped to his right calf. A Henry rifle rode in a saddle boot on the Ovaro outside.

Fargo drank the last of his coffee and said, "Man never knows when he's going to run into trouble."

"My motto, exactly!"

"Tell me more about Pearsoll," Fargo suggested. He hadn't really crossed swords with the man, so to speak, but he had the feeling Pearsoll might hold a grudge because of the way Fargo had interfered in his clash with the old man.

Before Olmsted could say anything, the Chinese man behind the counter shook his head and said, "Flynn Pearsoll bad man. Drink half the time, fight half the time, chase ladies half the time."

"That's three halves," Fargo pointed out with a grin.

"There plenty of Pearsoll to go 'round."

"Yeah, from the looks of him I'd say you might be right."

"He's killed four men in Gila City and the vicinity," Olmsted said solemnly. "That we know of."

"Are you saying I'd better watch my back?"

Olmsted shrugged his bony shoulders. "Not your back, necessarily. Pearsoll, to give credit where credit is due, generally shoots his victims from the front. That is, when he doesn't thrash the life out of them. That's happened on at least one occasion."

"I'm not in the habit of walking around scared," Fargo said. "But I'll keep my eyes open."

The door of the hash house opened behind them. Fargo glanced over his shoulder, then looked again at the two newcomers who hurried into the place.

He would have taken a second look at the two young women no matter where they were. They were that pretty. But here in these squalid surroundings, their beauty seemed even more striking.

No other series has this much historical action!

THE TRAILSMAN

Available wherever books are sold or at
www.penguin.com

Ralph
Cotton

JACKPOT RIDGE   21002-6
Jack Bell is a good gambler—so good that Early Philpot wants him
dead. But up in the mountains, Jack can outlast any lowlife posse Early
can rustle up. And he's willing to put them all to the test.

JUSTICE   19496-9
A powerful land baron uses his political influence to persuade local
lawmen to release his son from a simple assault charge. The young man,
however, is actually the leader of the notorious Half Moon Gang—a
mad pack of killers with nothing to lose!

BORDER DOGS   19815-8
The legendary Arizona Ranger Sam Burrack is forced to make the most
difficult decision of his life when his partner is captured by ex-
Confederate renegades—The Border Dogs. His only ally is a wanted
outlaw with blood on his hands...and a deadly debt to repay the Dogs.

BLOOD MONEY   20676-2
Bounty hunters have millions of reasons to catch J.T. Priest—but Marshal
Hart needs only one. And he's sworn to bring the killer down...mano-a-
mano.

DEVIL'S DUE   20394-1
The second book in Cotton's "Dead or Alive" series. *Los Pistoleros*
were the most vicious gang of outlaws around—but Hart and Roth
thought they had them under control...Until the jailbreak.

Available wherever books are sold or at
www.penguin.com